The Assassin

Honolulu

JIM WEST

ISBN
Hardcover: 978-1-965134-12-2
Paperback: 978-1-965134-11-5

Other Books by Jim West

DNAlien

DNAlien II

DNAlienIII

Genocide by GMO

Living Within a Strange Mind Volume I

Living Within a Strange Mind Volume II

The Making of an Assassin Atlanta

The Assassin Baltimore

The Assassin Chicago

The Assassin Denver

The Assassin El Paso

The Assassin Fort Worth

The Assassin Galveston

Chapter One

As American Airlines flight 1025 pulled to the Houston Intercontinental Airport (IAH) gate, First Officer Jim Lashley watched as Captain Rudy Jackson set the brakes and waited to shut down the remaining engine after ground electrical power was connected to the airplane.

"Parking checklist," Rudy said as he pulled his earpiece and microphone from his left ear, hanging it on the control wheel.

Jim quickly read each item on the list and watched Rudy complete each task.

As Jim said, "Parking checklist complete," mainly for the ever-listening cockpit voice recorder. Rudy stood and opened the cockpit door to say goodbye to the deplaning passengers.

Waiting in his seat for the plane to empty, Jim thought about what he would do with the four days he had off once they returned to the Dallas Fort Worth Airport (DFW).

As the last passenger entered the jet bridge and headed toward the terminal, Rudy took his hat from behind his seat and said, "I'll go down and take care of the walk-around since it's your leg back to DFW."

Jim grabbed his hat and replied, "I'll head up and get the paperwork. Anything I can get you while I'm up there?"

"A new contract doubling my pay and giving me twice as many days off would be nice," Rudy said, laughing. "Since I'm about to be divorced again, for the third time, I'm going to be a little strapped for cash," he continued as he stepped onto the jet bridge. "And I'll need the time off to search for the lucky number four."

"Not sure if I'd call the next one 'lucky number four' or not," Jim told him as he headed toward the gate agent's podium. "But I guess it would be correct to ask, 'Lucky for whom?' Perhaps you should reconsider the entire marriage since it appears you can't master the subtleties required for success."

"Wise advise, Grasshopper," Rudy responded, opening the door that led down to the ramp. "But the truth is that I like having a woman around when I return from a trip."

Pausing before stepping outside, he continued, "And since the first one got half, the second one only got half of the half I kept, the third one will only get half of the remaining quarter, which means it's getting cheaper each time. How can I not follow that financial plan?"

"How can all these highly paid financial planners not know this obvious road to economic success?" Jim joked, heading toward the terminal. "Surely one of the major companies like Charles Schwab would love to have you on their staff. Or maybe Harvard would like you to teach that philosophy in their financial doctoral program?"

"And share the secrets of my success?" Rudy replied as he headed downstairs. "Never! Let them learn the same way I did … from their mistakes."

Chapter Two

As Jim entered the terminal and stepped over to the gate agent's podium, he spotted an old friend sitting in one of the chairs facing the window, looking over the ramp.

Walking over, Jim said, "General, not to say it's ever a surprise to run into you in the most surprising places, but it's truly a surprise this time."

Gene stood smiling and extended his hand, saying, "It's never a surprise if you expect something to happen. And, after all these years, I'd expect you to expect just about anything."

Shaking his hand, Jim nodded and replied, "As always, your reasoning is as expected. Sooo… what brings you to Houston? Couldn't be just to see me because I'm sure you know that I'll be back in DFW in an hour or so." Jim said as he led Gene toward the gate agent's podium and started signing into the computer.

"I needed to see you and refuel the company jet," Gene told him. "This was a convenient place to accomplish both."

"And I guess Love Field wouldn't have worked just as well in an hour?" Jim asked as he pulled the flight data from the printer.

"Not really, since I also had some business here in Houston that I'll take care of after you leave," Gene answered. "Is there someplace we can have a little privacy?"

"Sure," Jim told him, nodding to the gate agent. "We can have a first-class to ourselves for a few minutes if that's all the time you'll need."

"That'll be fine," Gene said, following Jim to the jet bridge. "This shouldn't take more than a couple of minutes."

As they arrived at the airplane, Rudy was just coming in from inspecting the exterior for any apparent issues. "Hey, Jim," he said, spotting Gene. "Giving tours?"

"No," Jim answered as he introduced Gene to Rudy. "This is General Gene Barker. He was sort of my Commander during my first two tours in Vietnam. General, this is my Captain for the month, Rudy Jackson."

"At least he didn't say I'm sort of his Captain," Rudy said, smiling and shaking Gene's hand. "Good to meet you, General."

"Nice to meet you also, Captain," Gene replied. "And please, it's just Gene. I've long since forgone the title from our history together."

"And you may certainly call me Rudy," Rudy told him. "Jim seems to have trouble remembering that also."

"Too many years in the Marines," Gene remarked, nodding. "Salute it, call it sir, or shoot it. That's about all we could ever teach these guys. Maybe the airlines will tone him down just a bit."

"Here's the flight plan, Captain, sir," Jim said, shaking his head and handing Rudy the stack of papers for their return flight to DFW. "I've looked it over, and it appears to be satisfactory, sir. If there's nothing else, I believe the General has something he needs to discuss."

Rudy looked at Gene, smiling, and answered, "That'll be all, Mister Lashley. You're dismissed."

"Nice to meet you, Rudy," Gene said, shaking his hand again. "I'm not going to waste my time apologizing for Jim. He's too set in his old ways. But I do offer my condolences."

"Good to meet you too, Gene," Rudy told him. "The saving grace of the airlines is that each Captain only has to fly with him for a single month. Sort of our turn in the barrel, you might say."

"A month can be a lifetime," Gene replied, nodding as Jim headed for the first-class seating. "Just keep an eye on him. He's a great guy, just none too smart. Bless his little heart."

Chapter Three

"They'll start boarding soon," Jim said as he pointed to the first two seats on the left side of the airplane.

As Gene took the window seat, he pulled an envelope from the inside pocket of his jacket and handed it to Jim, saying, "I'd like for you to take a look at the names on this list when you get home.

I'm pretty sure you'll recognize most of them or at least be able to figure out who they are," Gene continued as Jim opened the envelope.

After taking a quick look, Jim answered, "A few Senators, some Congressmen I recognize, and some I don't think I've ever heard of."

Refolding the pages and replacing them in the envelope, he asked, "Just what am I looking for? Connections?"

"For now, just learn who these people are," Gene answered. "I've got to fly to Honolulu after I finish my business here, but I plan on being at Love Field around noon the day after tomorrow. I would greatly appreciate it if you could arrange to have the afternoon off."

"Not a problem," Jim said, laying the envelope in his lap. "Does this involve a Black Water contract?"

"Yes, but it's much more than most of our contracts," Gene acknowledged. "This is one of the only pro bono contracts I've ever known the company to take. So, yes, it's a Black Water contract. But I can't say much more than that for now. I'll give you the details when I see you in a couple of days if you're interested."

"Always interested," Jim said as Gene stood up. "Unless you have other plans for that evening, I'll see if I can get Marie's dad to cook something up for dinner."

"That sounds terrific," Gene told him as they headed back to the front of the plane. "And, you might just want to have the following day available. We have a meeting in New Orleans at ten o'clock that morning."

"You know I only have four days off after this flight, don't you?" Jim asked as they stopped by the cockpit.

"And I've only asked for your time on two of them," Gene retorted, smiling. "Is it so unpleasant that you have to put up with an old war buddy for a couple of days out of the year? Especially since I know you airline pilots actually only work three days a week."

Sticking his head into the cockpit, Gene said, "Rudy, very nice to meet you. Like I said, keep an eye on this one."

Rudy turned in his seat and said, "Good to meet you, too, Gene. Hope to see you again."

As they headed back up to the terminal, they met the flight attendants coming down the jet bridge, and the tall one in front smiled at Jim as they passed.

A few steps later, Jim looked at Gene's smile and quietly said, "No. Don't even think it."

"I wasn't going to say anything," Gene replied. "I just happened to notice how attractive the young lady was. Tall, slender, beautiful face, nice smile. Very attractive."

Gene glanced back over his shoulder and repeated, "Very attractive."

"Maybe you should stick to flying your private jet," Jim answered, shaking his head. "No distractions and no need for comments about the people I fly with."

"Just making small talk," Gene said as they came to the door that led to the terminal. "Guy stuff … noticing attractive ladies. Just guy stuff."

"Tell you what," Jim said as they entered the terminal, "I'll let you tell Marie all about your small talk regarding guy stuff over dinner."

Gene chuckled as Jim continued, "Not that it matters, but how long will the meeting in New Orleans take?"

"Probably only a couple of hours," Gene answered. "We should be back at Love Field by three or four at the latest."

"Will you be staying after that?" Jim asked as he noticed the gate agent opening the jet bridge door for the passengers.

"No," Gene answered as they moved from the doorway. "I've got to be back here in Houston that evening. We'll finish this discussion when I get back from Honolulu."

"Yes, sir," Jim said, shaking Gene's hand and turning toward the jet bridge. "See you then."

"Nice guy," Rudy said as Jim slid into his seat. "I guess you've known Gene for a long time."

"Years and years," Jim admitted as he picked up the sheets with their takeoff data and started setting up his instruments. "He's pretty much the reason I'm here today. Without his help, I'd probably be down there on the ramp tossing bags into the belly of the plane."

"Sounds like an interesting story," Rudy said as the gate agent poked her head into the cockpit. "Tell it to me. Maybe over a glass of tea on the next trip."

"Everyone's on board, Captain," the gate agent said, looking at Rudy. "Is it okay to close the door?"

"That'll be fine, Miss," Rudy told her. "I'll see you next trip down here."

Chapter Four

After landing at DFW, Jim said goodbye to Rudy and the flight attendants before boarding the tram that carried the employees from their parking lot to the terminals and back.

Once at his pickup, he tossed his suitcase in the passenger seat and headed for the North exit of the airport. As he drove east on 635 toward his home in Mesquite, he started thinking about the names he had seen on the list that was now secured in his suitcase.

Recognizing most as either Senators or Congressmen currently serving and a few from the news over the last few years, he wondered what all of these people had in common and why Black Water would be interested. Especially when Gene had said this was pro bono.

Even if Black Water took a contract for no pay, what role did Dark Water, the international enforcement arm, or Muddy Water, the domestic side with whom Jim was associated, have to play? Questions would have to wait until the day after tomorrow when Gene would be back from Hawaii.

Once home, he parked in the driveway and carried his suitcase into the house. Tossing it on the bed, he stripped off his uniform and hung his trousers and jacket in the closet. Removing the epaulets from his shirt, he put them on the next white shirt in line hanging in the closet.

After pulling on a pair of wranglers, a green knit shirt, and his Tony Lama boots, Jim took a Ziegen Bock from the refrigerator and headed for his favorite chair with the list of names in his hand.

Using his laptop computer, he searched each name even though he thought he recognized who the person was. Surprisingly, each of the names was easy to find. Ranging from Politicians to CEOs and even one prominent Pastor of the largest Baptist church in Dallas, Jim couldn't see a common thread to tie them together.

Taking a pen from the table beside his chair, he began making notations regarding each of the names. Starting with the most prominent, the Senators, he noted that the seven listed included five Democrats and two Republicans.

Then, he wrote the political party for each of the 25 congressmen. The list contained fifteen Democrats and ten Republicans. Next, he noted that there were two females on the list of 32 politicians.

Continuing to search the internet, he built a rough picture of men and women of power. But there wasn't a single issue that he could find that would bring these people to the attention of Black Water.

In his position within Muddy Water, which usually involved eliminating people domestically for various reasons, he couldn't see why Gene would have him researching this particular group.

Finally leaving the list on the table, Jim took his empty beer back to the kitchen and took another from the refrigerator. Taking a sip, he dialed Marie's number to let her know that he was back in town and hoped that she would want to get together for the evening.

As she answered, he said, "Marie, so good to hear your voice. How's your week been?"

"Rather hectic," Marie answered. "Dad had a small issue at the restaurant involving a kitchen fire. The biggest issue was Mom telling him to start being more careful."

"Was anyone hurt?" Jim asked with concern in his voice.

"No, a little smoke on the ceiling, but it just joined what's been accumulating there over the last fifteen years," Marie answered. "Dad's eyebrows were a little singed along with some hair on his arms as he tried to put it out with a rag he had in his back pocket. Dad had dropped a kitchen towel too close to a lit burner. When it ignited, he tried to put it out. One of the kitchen staff called the fire department as soon as he saw the flames. Of course, Mom came running into the kitchen when she heard everyone yelling and saw Dad slapping at the burning towel with his hands and a rag. All she saw was the flames and smoke," Marie finished. "I think the sight of Dad without eyebrows was what concerned her the most."

"I can imagine," Jim said, smiling. "Just don't tell me your mom used her eyeliner to draw some eyebrows on your dad's face."

"Oh no," Marie answered, laughing. "Dad wouldn't allow that to happen. By the way, how was your trip?"

"Same as always," Jim answered. "Take 150 people from DFW to XYZ. Then, 150 more to PDQ. Then 150 more somewhere and spend the night. Get up the next morning take 150 somewhere, and get another 150 going where I just left. Spend the night and bring 150 strangers back here. Or some combination of the above."

"And I always thought being an airline pilot would be exciting," Marie remarked.

"Hours and hours of boredom punctuated by moments of utter boredom is a better description," Jim corrected. "But I did run into Gene down in Houston before I came home today. That's about as exciting as anything on the trip."

"How's he doing?" Marie asked.

"Same as always," Jim answered. "He was down in Houston for something and was leaving this afternoon for Honolulu."

"I'm guessing he didn't invite you to go with him," Marie observed.

"No, but he did say he was coming back through here in two days and I offered to see if your dad might be able to cook up something for dinner that night," Jim told her.

"I'm sure he can," Marie said. "And, if you're interested, I'm pretty sure he'd be glad to cook dinner for us tonight."

"That sounds great," Jim replied. "After hotel or airline food for the last few days, I'm ready for something else. Shall I come get you?"

"I'll just meet you there," she answered. "I've got some running around to do before then. How about meeting me there at about seven?"

"Sounds good," Jim said before hanging up. "I'll see you then."

Chapter Five

Later, after a quick shower, Jim headed for Siciliano's 'A Taste of Italy' restaurant in Garland. Even as he headed north with the dwindling traffic, it was hard to pay attention and watch for the errant drivers who were constantly changing lanes without any signal and usually trying to make it across the highway to an exit at the last moment. The list kept running through his head, and he knew it would be on his mind until he had a chance to meet with Gene.

Arriving at Siciliano's, he saw Marie's car parked beside her dad's car. Pulling into the open spot beside her, Jim took a quick look at the time and breathed a sigh of relief that he was ten minutes early. Years of military and airline work made him almost paranoid about being late.

Entering the restaurant, Marie's mother, Aurora, met him at the door and gave him a hug, saying, "Jim, it's so good to see you again. How was your flight?"

Hugging her back, he answered, "Just another day in paradise. I understand you guys had a little excitement while I was gone."

"It was nothing," she answered as she led him to the back room. "Just a little kitchen fire. Not the first and probably not the last."

"I'm glad nobody got hurt, other than some singed hair," Jim replied, smiling as he saw Marie setting a bottle of wine on their table.

"I guess Marie told you about that," Aurora said as she looked at her daughter.

"She mentioned it," Jim answered as Marie came over and took his arm.

"Jim's practically family," Marie said, kissing his cheek. "Besides, he would have noticed Dad's missing eyebrows anyway."

"Still, you know your father doesn't like anyone to know that he occasionally makes a mistake," Aurora said as she surveyed the table. "You two sit down, and I'll let Anthony know you're here."

"How are the girls?" Jim asked as Marie poured two glasses of wine.

"They're fine," Marie answered, handing one of the glasses to Jim. "Seems like there's always something happening up there in Denton to keep them occupied."

"That's college for you," Jim agreed as they tapped their glasses. "At least they're close enough to come home if they get bored with the constant parties, football games, or whatever they find to keep them busy when they aren't studying."

"What about you when you're not off flying around the skies?" Marie asked, taking a sip of her wine. "What do you do to keep busy?"

"Clean house, do laundry, mow the yard, wash the car, all that exciting stuff," Jim answered. "It's amazing how little time it seems I have when I get home from a trip before it's time to go again."

"When are you going out again?" she asked as they saw her dad coming back to their table.

"Four days off," Jim told her as he rose to greet Anthony.

"Tony, so nice of you to take time off to come see us," Jim said, shaking his hand.

"Always a pleasure to come to see you," Tony told him, smiling. "And, of course, I never get to see my beautiful daughter enough.

Aurora, bring a couple of more glasses," he yelled over his shoulder. "I've got a few minutes before I have to return to that blazing inferno called a kitchen."

"I heard about the inferno," Jim said, laughing. "And I can see that you managed to face the challenge."

"So, you noticed," Tony said, joining in on the laughter. "I'm thinking of shaving my head like that guy who advertises those cleaner things. You know, Mr. Clean."

"Probably wouldn't work," Jim replied, shaking his head. "That guy had eyebrows. White, but he had eyebrows."

"Another great idea shot down," Tony said as Aurora arrived. "Maybe I'll just let my eyebrows grow and look like that guy, Groucho Marx."

"Oh, no, you don't," Aurora said, setting the glasses on the table. "You look enough like him with that mustache anyway."

Tony took the glass of wine Marie had poured, wiggled his missing eyebrows up and down, and pantomimed, holding a cigar, saying, "Ah, my little chickadee."

"I believe you're mixing up Groucho and W. C. Fields," Jim said, laughing.

"You could be right," Tony said, taking a seat. "So, tell me. What would you like for dinner tonight? Some of my just fine lasagna again?"

"I guess you'll never let me forget that, will you?" Jim asked, holding up his glass for a toast.

"Never," Tony said as Aurora took a seat beside Marie. "So, what would you like tonight?"

"How about shrimp alfredo?" Jim suggested.

"As you wish," Tony said, nodding. "I'll have it right out. Marie, how about you?"

"Shrimp alfredo sounds good to me, too," she answered as he finished his wine.

"Excellent," Tony said, setting his empty glass on the table and standing. "Aurora, when you finish your wine, please come get a plate of brochette for the kids while I prepare their meal."

Chapter Six

When dinner was finished, the table cleared, and Marie poured the last of the wine into Jim's glass, asking, "Would you like to come over tonight? I got a very special movie I think you'd like."

"Sounds good," Jim answered, taking his glass from her hand. "What's the movie?"

"Is that important?" Marie asked with a quizzical look. "I thought just being with me would be enough."

"Of course, being with you is enough," Jim answered quickly. "I was just wondering what movie you thought I'd like. It would be hard to beat the first movie you brought to my house. Dr. Strangelove. Now, that was great. And a hell of a surprise."

"I'm just teasing," Marie replied, smiling. "But I thought the movie Airplane would be right up there with your sense of humor and the fact that you were a Marine aviator and an airline pilot.

By the way, why are Navy and Marine pilots called aviators instead of pilots like the Air Force?" she asked as she finished her wine.

"I believe it has something to do with the term pilot," Jim answered. "There are certain people that move the ships in and out of ports or waterways that are called pilots. Calling our pilots aviators prevents any confusion. At least, that's the best reason I can think of. And, a Marine aviator includes anyone involved with flying, such as the navigator or weapons system operator. The pilot would refer specifically to the person actually flying the plane."

"Sounds reasonable," Marie replied, smiling as she set her empty glass on the table. "I just thought it was because you wanted to be different from either the Army or the Air Force. Now I know it wasn't some petty issue; you didn't want to be confused with someone who merely drives a boat."

After telling Tony and Aurora goodbye, Jim followed Marie to her house thankful that he had decided to drive the 'Vette instead of his old pickup. Parking on the curb, he joined her as she unlocked the front door.

"Want anything to drink while we watch the movie?" she asked as they entered the living room.

"A Jack and Coke would be appropriate since I don't have to drive home," Jim said as Marie put her arms around his waist.

Stepping back, she said, "I invited you to a movie. What makes you think that included spending the night?"

"I have a sixth sense about these things," Jim said, pulling her back. "It's a gift."

"Oh, now you're gifted," Marie replied, putting her arms around his neck. "Then tell me, what am I thinking about now?"

"You're wondering how a dumbassed country boy like me ever came into your life," he told her, kissing the top of her head. "Or, you're wondering how many Jack and Cokes you'll have to serve me trying to lure me into your bedroom."

"You know, you truly are gifted," Marie said playfully, slapping his shoulder. "That is if gifted is synonymous with delusional. Now, if you'll go mix your drink, I'll get the movie ready and join you on the couch."

"Would you like anything?" Jim asked, turning toward the kitchen.

"Jack and Coke sounds good to me," she answered as she turned on the TV and CD player. "About one-half as strong as you make yours, so I'll be sober enough to lure you into my lair after the movie."

Later, as the movie was ending, Marie asked, "So, is that a true depiction of the airline life? You can tell me. I'm good at keeping secrets."

"I'll say this about Airplane," Jim answered as he stood. "Airplane is closer to airline life than Top Gun is to the life of a fighter pilot."

"You mean the girls don't swoon over you when you walk into the Officer's Club wearing your spanking white uniform and gold wings?" Marie joked, turning off the TV.

"Oh, that part is true," Jim said in mock serious-ness. "And now when I walk into the hotel bar in my crisply starched white shirt with three silver stripes on the epaulets, it's déjà vu all over again, to quote Yogi Berra."

"Right," Marie said, taking their glasses to the kitchen. "You forget that you told me you never go into the bar on a layover. Especially in uniform. Company rules about drinking … "

"I'm only there for a glass of iced tea," Jim countered as they headed for the bedroom. "And at the bequest of the Captain."

Chapter Seven

After going to Denny's for breakfast the next morning, Jim took Marie back to her house, and they made arrangements for dinner at Jim's that evening.

Once back home, Jim spent the rest of the morning doing laundry, cleaning the house, and all the mundane chores necessary to make sure the house would be presentable when Marie came.

Seeing that he needed a few items from the grocery store, he grabbed his uniform to take to the cleaners and headed out the door.

When he returned home a couple of hours later, there was a plain brown envelope lying on the mat at the front door. Unlocking the door, he carried the groceries to the kitchen and returned to get the envelope.

Grabbing a knife from the kitchen, Jim sat at the dining table and looked at both sides of the envelope to see if there were any markings or hints as to who had left it.

Seeing nothing, he slid the knife blade into the end of the envelope where it had been sealed. After opening it, Jim removed a single sheet of paper and laid it on the table.

Looking back inside to make sure there wasn't anything else, he put the envelope to the side and picked up the sheet.

Centered above the first paragraph was a single word. TREASON. The paragraph read: The offense of attempting by overt act to overthrow the government of the state to which the offender owes allegiance or to kill or personally injure the sovereign or the sovereign's family. Giving aid and comfort to enemies either on U.S. or foreign soil, an act punishable by death.

The word SEDITION was centered next above a single sentence which read: Incitement of resistance to or insurrection against lawful authority.

INSURRECTION was then centered above another sentence reading: An act or instance of revolting against civil authority or an established government.

REVOLUTION followed suit, and the sentence below read: Attempting to make a major change in a government.

COUP was next, and below it, the sentence read: A sudden decisive exercise of force in politics and especially the overthrow or alteration of an existing government by a small group: coup d'etat.

Then, in bold italics, the words PUNISHABLE BY DEATH were centered at the bottom of the page.

Jim had no doubt that the envelope had something to do with the list of names he had been researching, as well as no doubt who had the envelope delivered to this house.

Even with this new information, he failed to see anything that would tie the names together. Granted, the majority of the names were politicians, but from his readings, he didn't see any way they could be planning an overthrow of the government.

Then, there were the names of the CEOs of major corporations. How did they figure in the implied conspiracy? And a Baptist preacher? Not only did this not help, it made it even more confusing.

How would such a diverse group possibly form with the goal of upending the government of the United States? This just didn't make sense.

Bringing the original list of names back to the table, Jim reread each name and the notes he had made while researching them. Impossible. The diversity between these people made such an idea impossible.

Even the different committees the senators and congressmen chaired or served on couldn't be tied to anything approaching a conspiracy.

Then Jim decided that he was looking at it from the wrong perspective. These people weren't the ones the note referred to. It could only be any actions Black Water was planning.

However, knowing Gene and having worked with Black Water for several years made that seem absurd as well. There was something missing. All he had were pieces of the puzzle, and it was doubtful if he'd have access to the full picture until tomorrow when Gene arrived.

Then there was the trip to New Orleans. How was that figured into the mystery? Maybe even Gene wasn't fully aware of what this involved.

Looking at his watch, Jim realized that he still needed to take a shower and put on clean clothes before Marie arrived. Gathering the pages together and putting them all in the envelope, he took them to his bedroom and placed the envelope on the top shelf in his closet.

Chapter Eight

The following morning, after Marie had left, Jim retrieved the envelope and started looking closer at all of the names … in particular, the Senators and Congressmen.

Doing a deep background search, some oddities began to emerge. Minor offenses, but nothing that could be construed as a reason to eliminate them. Numerous occasions where they had misled the public, but that seemed to be the norm for politicians across the spectrum.

Various rumors regarding sexual harassment, payoffs, questionable business dealings, and stock trades that bordered on insider information were numerous as well. All told, it amounted to a group of people who thought they were above what a moral person would believe as appropriate behavior, but apparently, no laws had been broken. At least not that Jim could find.

It was times like this when he wished he had access to the computers back at Black Water headquarters. And more specifically, access to Bracer and her team of computer nerds. That group could find every aspect of a person's life in ten seconds. Even as far back as what diapers they wore and how often they needed changing.

He had just started digging into the preacher's background when the doorbell rang. Closing down the computer and gathering the papers, he slid them back into the envelope and put them beneath his laptop.

Opening the door, Gene smiled and asked, "Surprised?"

"Not really," Jim said, shaking his outstretched hand. "You did tell me you were coming by today. Or is old age and forgetfulness sneaking up on you?"

"My mind is a steel trap," Gene countered, setting his briefcase on the table beside Jim's computer as Jim led him into the kitchen. "The only problem is that after all these years, there is so much information in there that it may take a second or two to find it."

"Sounds like you need a new filing system," Jim said, taking two cups down. "Or some rust remover since steel does rust in a moist, dark environment. Coffee?"

"Sure," Gene answered, glancing around. "Looks like someone had a visitor last night."

"What makes you think that?" Jim asked, handing him his cup.

"Probably because there are two coffee cups in the sink," Gene answered, smiling.

"One from yesterday and another this morning?" Jim posed as he led Gene to the table.

"Nope," Gene countered. "I know your habits. Nothing is left in the sink when you go to bed. So don't try to hide anything from me. I know you too well." He smiled knowingly. "Now, let's get down to why I'm really here, shall we?"

"Please, have a seat," Jim said, taking his chair in front of his computer.

Pulling the envelope from beneath it, he passed the sheet that had TREASON on the top and asked, "I don't suppose you know how this came to rest on my porch?"

Gene took the sheet and replied, "I don't know the person's name that left it there, but I know the person who had it delivered."

"And, just who would that be?" Jim asked, taking the sheet back from Gene.

"The person we're going to meet tomorrow morning in New Orleans," Gene answered. "But, before we get into that, what have you discovered about the names on the list?"

"Pretty much what a normal person would find searching the internet," Jim answered, taking the sheet with the names and passing it to Gene.

"A group of entitled slime balls," he continued as Gene read the notes along with each name. "Nothing that I can see that would indicate a reason for Black Water or us, Muddy Water, to be involved."

Pausing until Gene looked up, Jim then added, "Especially since the issue of treason or coup seems to be involved with this operation."

Nodding, Gene handed the sheet back to Jim and took another from his briefcase. Giving it to Jim, he said, "This is who we're meeting tomorrow. I'm sure you know who he is."

"Senator Jackson Knowles, from Louisiana," Jim answered, looking at the picture. "His name wasn't on the list, as you well know."

"No, it isn't," Gene said, taking the picture back and replacing it in his briefcase.

Gene leaned back in his chair, studying Jim for a second, and then asked, "What do you think the 'Treason' message meant?"

"At first, I thought it meant that those people were planning something," Jim answered. "But there weren't any connections and such a diverse group could never plan something such as a government takeover without knowledge spread across the headline of every newspaper in the country. Then, I decided that it had to mean that what Black Water was planning, eliminating such a large group of politicians, was a more likely answer," he continued.

"Then, I discounted that because I knew Black Water wouldn't be involved. But mainly, I discounted it because I knew you'd never be involved in it. And I know you know I wouldn't either," Jim finished.

"You're right about that," Gene said as he rose to refill his coffee. "But, it's more complicated than that. As you just said, neither the company, me, nor you would sign on to anything close to treason or sanction a coup d'etat."

"Okay, then, what are we talking about?" Jim asked, following Gene.

"There's this little inconvenience that is why those people's names are on that list," Gene answered, leaning back against the counter.

"And what is this little inconvenience that measures up to treason?" Jim asked.

Gene took a couple of sips and finally said, "The little inconvenience is that there are videos of all of those people involved with a sex trafficking ring."

Chapter Nine

Stunned, Jim finally asked, "All of them?"

"And one more that became the catalyst for what we are going to be working with," Gene answered. "This has been going on for a while, but it's reached such a point that something must be done."

"Who knows about this?" Jim asked, heading back to the table. "How high up does this go?"

"As to who knows, very few," Gene told him, taking his seat. "As to how high up this goes … to the very top."

"You've got to be kidding me," Jim replied, spilling some of his coffee on the table. "You're saying our…"

"Yes, that's what I'm saying," Gene told him, nodding. "Now, here are some basic guidelines for this program. First, I'm going to destroy any paper evidence. And we're going to do the same with your computer. I've got another one for you in the car. Bracer added some special programs to ensure it can't be hacked," Gene said as he reached for the three sheets of paper lying on the table. "And names will never be mentioned again once the operation starts."

"How will we communicate regarding the targets if they are indeed targets," Jim asked as he watched Gene put the papers in his briefcase.

"You'll be given a card that looks exactly like a credit card that allows access to a special program on your computer. By the way, the card actually is a credit card from a bank belonging to a customer of Dark Water. Just don't use it," Gene answered. "That computer program will have encoded directions and instructions. Those instruct-ions will come from either me or this person," he finished, holding up the picture of Senator Knowles. "He will be using the initials 'IL' in any communication. Mine will be 'FC.'"

"What about those other names?" Jim asked. "And me?"

"The names of the list will be identified by a number," Gene answered. "The program has a random number generator and assigns that number, which changes based on the code you'll receive in the text.

For example, if the code is afternoon, and it's always the second word in the third paragraph, the list of names will reorganize according to the random number generator," he explained.

"So, you use your card to open the program, see the second word in the third paragraph, and type it in as a reply," Gene elaborated. "That then provides the list organized by number with the initials."

"What initials are you referring to?" Jim asked. "Yours? His? Mine?"

"All of us," Gene said, nodding. "The initials are the letter preceding the first letter in the first name and the letter following the first letter of the last name.

The letter preceding my first name, Gene, is F. The letter following my last name, Barker, is C," Gene finished. "I'm sure you didn't spend a lot of time memorizing the names, so the program will provide a list corresponding to the names once you send the encrypted initials in a reply as you did with the code word."

"All of this just to deal with a bunch of politicians, a couple of CEOs, and a preacher or two?" Jim asked, shaking his head. "Why not just turn the tapes over to CNN or NBC? Let the chips fall where they may."

"One of the constrictions placed on us by IL," Gene answered. "He'll elaborate more tomorrow when we're in person. By the way, I'm sure you're familiar with a SCIF, a sensitive compartmented information facility."

"Yeah, I've used them," Jim answered as he reached over and took a picture of Senator Knowles out of the briefcase. "Now I'm starting to wonder if I really want to be involved. I hope IL has some very persuasive arguments tomorrow. This is starting to sound like one of the most FUBAR operations I've ever dealt with."

Chapter Ten

"What time does Marie want us to meet at the restaurant?" Gene asked, taking his empty coffee cup to the kitchen.

"I told her I'd call after you got here," Jim answered, following him. "I'll tell her seven o'clock."

Looking at his watch, Gene suggested, "Looks like we have a few hours before we need to get ready; what say we go have lunch?"

"Sounds good to me," Jim said, rinsing both cups out and putting them in the dishwasher. "Anywhere in particular?"

"Anywhere besides Denny's" Gene said laughing. "You've taken me to every Denny's within a five-state area. I'll wager that you've already been to Denny's since you got back from your last trip. Pick something new."

"Well, there is this place I just heard about," Jim said, shaking his head. "They are only open for breakfast or lunch. If we go now, we can probably make it before they close."

"Well, hell. Let's get there before you change your mind," Gene said, making sure he had all of the sheets of paper in his briefcase before closing it. "I'll drive since you probably want to take the 'Vette with the top down."

"It would be more fun than your standard Suburban with blacked-out windows," Jim said, following Gene out of the house.

"Some other day," Gene said, tossing his briefcase in the rear seat. "Now, where do I go?"

"Head back over to 635 and go north," Jim directed, getting into the passenger seat. "You'll take the exit for Towne Centre Drive and go north until reaching North Town East Blvd, then east to West Emporium Circle, about a quarter of a mile. Take a left on Emporium and then left on Pavillion Court."

"Just don't let me get lost," Gene said as he started the car. "Now, the reason I was in Honolulu was to set up the operation regarding the sex trafficking ring.

It's based down in Brazil, and I'm letting Dark Water handle that end." Gene explained heading for 635.

"But here's how it works. They basically build a portfolio of available cabin attendants. Once they learn what the client is interested in, age, gender, size, or whatever, they allow him or her to select the attendants they want for their cruise.

The ship, named the Barco Do Amor, is a 250-foot yacht with a crew of ten, including the Captain, deck hands, Chef, and all the others required to keep the ship at sea," Gene said as they joined 635 heading north.

"It costs the customer $10,000 per day, five-day minimum, to charter the ship," he continued as he merged with the traffic.

"That's just for the ship; it's another thousand dollars a day for each cabin attendant," he explained, trying to move out of the exit lane. "You can do the math and see that most of us couldn't afford to take a tour of the ship if it was in port."

"Where do they get the cabin attendants," Jim asked.

"South America, Thailand, the Philippines, all over the world," Gene answered as he saw a sign for his exit five miles ahead.

"How old are these attendants?" Jim asked, wondering how all of the people on the list could afford such an expense, even without the cabin attendants.

"Varies," Gene said, shaking his head. "But, from what we've discovered, I'd say twelve to fifteen is the normal range. Both boys and girls."

"How many cabin attendants do they usually have?" Jim asked, watching the road for cars entering from the access road.

"Our preacher had four, all fourteen years old, all from Mexico," Gene told him. "Stayed out for the five-day minimum."

"Seventy thousand dollars," Jim exclaimed. "I wonder how many of his congregation knew what their tithes were buying? Probably told them he was on missionary duty, and it was an annual ritual he had pledged to uphold."

"Let's not forget the other religions," Gene said, maneuvering to take the upcoming exit. "Everyone's heard about the priests and the choirboys. Well, there just happens to be an Archdiocese that has outdone them all."

"What is Black Water turning into?" Jim asked as they exited 635. "A morality enforcement unit? Again, I ask, why not just turn this over to the news media?"

"Just be patient, grasshopper," Gene told him as they saw Towne East Blvd approaching. "I think you'll understand after IL lays out the big picture. I had my doubts, but having seen the impact releasing this information would have, I made my decision to work on the problem.

But it'll be your decision regarding your participation. And I assure you, it won't have any impact on your career with Black Water," Gene said, turning left on West Emporium. "I think I know what your decision will be, but it's just that … your decision."

Chapter Eleven

Gene and Jim walked in after parking at the Seven Mile Café and were immediately led to a table. "Sort of slow this morning?" Jim asked as he took his seat.

"Not really," the waitress said, handing them menus. "Our breakfast rush is over, and it's a shade early for the lunch bunch. What would you gentlemen like to drink?"

"Unsweet iced tea for me," Gene said, looking at his menu.

"Same, please," Jim told her. "With lemon, please."

"I'll be right back," she said, scribbling on her order pad.

"This looks pretty good," Gene remarked, looking at the breakfast menu.

"Not bad," Jim agreed. "I'd order the Huevos Rancheros, but I've had some of the best down in San Antonio at Mi Tierra and at H3 in Fort Worth. I'd compare them and I doubt they will live up to the other places, so I'll try the Papas Rancheras instead."

"I'll order the Huevos Rancheros and let you know," Gene told him as the waitress set their drinks down.

"I guess you guys are ready to order?" she asked, looking at Jim.

"I'd like the Papas Rancheras," Jim answered. "And a side of Pico de Gallo and a couple of flour tortillas, please."

"You got it, sweetheart," she said before turning to Gene. "And for you, sir?"

"I'd like the Huevos Rancheros," Gene told her, handing her his menu. "And please, put both on a single ticket for me."

As she walked away, Gene picked up his tea and asked, "Do you know that you just ordered a female meal?"

"What makes you say that?" Jim asked with a quizzical look.

"In Spanish, the male version ends in an 'o' while the female version ends in an 'a'," he answered. "Huevos Rancheros … male. Papas Rancheras … female."

"Do you speak fluent Russian?" Jim asked, shaking his head.

"Not really," Gene answered. "Just a few words."

"Stick with the Russian," Jim told him. "You don't know *caca* about Spanish. For example, what is the Spanish word for masculine?"

"Just a guess, but *masculino*?" Gene answered.

"You would be correct," Jim told him, watching his face. "Now, what about for feminine?"

"Feminina," Gene answered.

"You'd be wrong, sir," Jim said laughing. "The correct word for feminine is *femenino*. Your *'male is an 'o' and female is an 'a' rule'* isn't always correct. You'd be misgendering if you use that in every circumstance."

"Hey, at least I know that *Papas* doesn't mean Papas, as in the Mamas and Papas," Gene replied joining in laughing. "More like Mr. Potato Head."

"But *Mamas* is still Mamas," Jim added as the waitress arrived with their meals. "Guess the group would have been the Mothers and Potatoes."

"You guys seem to be having a good time," she remarked, setting their meals in front of them. "Enjoy, and let me know if there's anything else I can do for you."

After taking a bite, Jim nodded and said, "Pretty damn good. How's the Huevos Rancheros?"

"I'd have to give them a nine out of ten," Gene said, wiping his mouth.

"Why not a ten out of ten?" Jim asked as he loaded a tortilla with black beans, chorizo, cheese, avocado, and cilantro jalapeno sauce.

"Because if I gave them a ten and found something better, how would I grade those?" Gene answered breaking the eggs and stirring in the cheese and pulled pork.

"Ten plus seems available," Jim remarked, putting a spoonful of Pico de Gallo on his eggs. "Wiggle room, so to speak."

"An interesting concept," Gene agreed, using a tortilla to hold a spoonful of black beans, hollandaise sauce, and some Pico de Gallo.

After a few minutes of enjoying his meal, Jim asked, "So, not to turn to business, but what's going to happen to the *Love Boat* when we start this game?"

"That, my dear boy, will become your problem," Gene answered, taking a sip of tea.

"I thought you said the operation was based in Brazil," Jim argued. "That would make it a Dark Water problem."

"The *sex ring* operation is based in Brazil," Gene corrected him. But the yacht is based out of Honolulu. So is the crew. That's the reason I went there. If tomorrow goes as I'm guessing, you'll have plenty of time to work on that issue while we muddle through what IL has in mind. Ready to go?”

“Sure thing, *FC*, as soon as the lady brings you our check,” Jim answered, finishing his glass of tea and wiping his mouth. “And thank the company for buying, once again.”

Chapter Twelve

After spending the afternoon discussing the people involved and the depth of Black Water's investigations for the past year, Jim and Gene headed to the restaurant to meet Marie.

As they entered, Aurora met them at the door, looked at Gene, and exclaimed, "My word, Signore Barker, you've come back to see us. Welcome. Welcome. Let me guide you to your table."

"Thank you, Aurora," Gene replied with a slight bow. "But only if you'll call me Gene."

"Of course, *Gene*," she said, turning to look at him. "My apologies. Now, Marie is back in the kitchen helping her father. I'll go tell her you're here and let her take care of you."

"Now I'm hurt," Jim said, following Aurora to the table in the rear. "You welcome Gene, and pay me no attention. None at all."

"You know you're always welcome," she said as they arrived at the table, and she gave Jim a quick hug. "I just wanted Gene to know that we always appreciate his time with us when he comes to town."

"A visit to your restaurant is always at the top of my list," Gene told her. "Any time I get a chance to come down and visit my friend, Jim, I make him bring me here for a most delicious meal. And to visit your family. Always a pleasure."

"Thank you," Aurora replied. "Now, you two have a seat, and Marie will be right out to take care of you."

As she headed back to get Marie, Gene turned to Jim and asked, "What do you think Anthony will be making for us tonight?"

"Not a clue," Jim answered, looking around the restaurant. "I know Marie told him I was coming, but I'm not sure if she told him you'd be with me."

"I'm sure she did," Gene replied as they saw Marie approaching their table with a bottle of wine and three glasses.

Standing as she arrived, Gene said, "Marie, so very nice to see you again."

"Thank you, Gene," she told him as she set the wine and glasses on the table. "I'm so glad you got a chance to come visit us again."

"And always happy to see you," Marie told Jim, giving him a quick hug. "You guys take your seats, and I'll be right back with some bread while we wait for Dad to finish cooking."

"What's Tony cooking for us tonight?" Gene asked as he poured the wine.

"I'll let him surprise you," she said, turning to leave. "Dad likes to surprise his guests."

A few minutes later, Marie returned with a platter of steaming bread and melted garlic butter. Setting it on the table, she said, "Dad will be back here in a few minutes with your meals. I'll join you when he does. In the meantime, enjoy the bread. Dad just made it."

"My mom used to make bread," Jim said, taking a slice of it and dipping it in the melted butter. "I loved the smell when I came into the house. I think it was because of the yeast.

Anyway, there was nothing better than a thick slice of that warm bread with a ton of butter and a glass of cold milk," Jim finished, taking a bite. "Don't you dare tell Tony I said it, but Mom's bread puts this to shame."

"If he knew, your little slur regarding his lasagna would be a wrist slap in comparison," Gene said, dipping a slice in the butter. "Not to mention, he'd probably toss both of us into the street, and I'd never get to eat here again."

"What's this about never getting to eat here again?" Tony said as he led Marie and Aurora to their table, carrying a tray with a large covered bowl and three plates.

"I was just telling Jim that I hope he never gets transferred to another base, or I'd have no reason to come to Garland," Gene quickly answered.

"Oh, are you about to be transferred?" Tony asked as Marie set the tray down.

"No," Jim answered as Aurora set the covered bowl and three plates around the table. "Even if I had to transfer to another base for a chance to upgrade to Captain, I'd still live in Mesquite. I'd just commute to wherever I was based for my flights and return when I finished."

"Well, we don't want you ever to leave," Tony said as Marie sat next to Jim. "Now, you enjoy the meal, and I'll come join you for a glass of wine when you're done."

Chapter Thirteen

As Marie removed the cover from the bowl, Gene asked, "Do you know what this is, Marie?"

Marie smiled, taking a large serving spoon and fork from the tray. "It is Daddy's clam and mussel linguini. Now, I'll serve if you'd pass me your plate."

After everyone's plate was filled, Jim raised his wine glass. "To our host!"

"To our host!" Marie and Gene parroted as they clinked glasses.

"Now, normally, the clams and mussels are served in their shells," Marie pointed out as Gene took a forkful of the linguini. "But he removed the meat for tonight to make it less, let's say, messy. And we don't need a separate bowl for the shells."

"This is good!" Jim said, nodding. "I mean, really good. And I'm glad Tony left the shells in the kitchen. I always hated trying to get every little bit of the clam out. And then the shells ..."

"Guess I'll have to try to make it back here more often," Gene said as he dug into the pile of linguini on his plate. "As Jim says, this is *just fine*."

"Oh, no," Marie said, laughing. "Let's not start that again. At least not where Daddy can hear it."

"Hear what?" Tony said, walking to the table. "What's *Daddy* not supposed to hear?"

"It's my fault, Tony," Jim said, trying to stop laughing. "Gene's making fun of one of my earlier comments after I said this is really good. And I'll add, best in the Metroplex."

"Guilty," Gene replied, wiping his mouth and shaking his head. "I referred to Jim's *just fine* comment purely in jest. This is truly a masterpiece of culinary art."

"Aurora, bring my biggest cooking spoon!" Tony yelled over his shoulder. "It's time for the most famous of all Italian traditions … the vendetta!"

"What's this about a big spoon?" Aurora asked, coming to the table. "Why do you need a spoon?"

"It's nothing," Tony said, laughing. "I was just discussing the vendetta for insulting my cooking skills, but our guests have suddenly developed an appreciation for my *fine* meal preparations. Forget the spoon. Bring us a bottle of *Disaronno* and five glasses."

Pulling out a chair, Tony asked, "Gene, Marie tells me you just got back from Honolulu; how was it?"

"Beautiful country, perfect weather, but not enough time to enjoy either," Gene answered as he prepared to take another bite. "My job takes me to some great places, but mostly, I get to see the inside of a car, a hotel, or a boardroom in some office building."

"Sounds like Jim's description of his job," Tony said, nodding. "Every tourist destination you can imagine, but when all you see is the hotel room, you might as well stay home."

"It's just that they don't pay me to stay home," Jim added as Aurora brought the *Disaronno* and five crystal liqueur glasses. "But sometimes I get a couple of hours to see the city. I like going to Mexico City. There's a great museum just a couple of blocks from the hotel. And, there are a couple of art museums in Chicago that are close enough to visit," as he got another forkful of the linguini.

"Maybe someday, you can accompany Marie back to Italy," Tony said. "Maybe someday Aurora and I can take all of you and the kids to see where my family comes from. I think it's important to stay in touch with your roots."

"Now that I'd enjoy," Jim replied, looking at Marie. "Just let me know when."

"What do you have planned for tomorrow?" Tony asked Gene as he topped off his glass.

"I need to be in New Orleans tomorrow morning for a few hours," Gene answered. "As a matter of fact, I need to take Jim with me. I'm meeting with a new customer, and I'd like to have Jim there in case there are issues that he is more familiar with than I."

"Will you be staying in here when you get back tomorrow?" Marie asked, placing her fork on the empty plate in front of her.

"Unfortunately, I have to be back in Quantico tomorrow evening, or I'd stay just to come back here for dinner," Gene replied.

"Well, if things change, we'd love to see you and Jim again tomorrow," Tony said, standing. "But, for now, I must go tend the fires. It's amazing how food doesn't get cooked while I'm out here."

Gene rose and shook Tony's hand, saying, "I'm just glad you're in there cooking when I come. I'm looking forward to seeing you again."

Chapter Fourteen

The next morning at nine o'clock, as Jim arrived at Love Field, he saw Gene and a man wearing an airline Captain's uniform standing in the Business Jet operations area. Walking up to them, he said, "Good morning, Gene. Hope I didn't keep you waiting."

"Good morning, Jim," Gene replied, turning to shake his hand. "This is Robert Sproc. He'll be our Captain for the trip to New Orleans and back."

"Nice to meet you, Rob," Jim shook his hand.

"You, too," Rob replied. "Paul, our Co-pilot, is finishing his walk-around inspection, and we'll be ready to go as soon as the fuel truck is finished."

"If it's all right with you, Jim and I will go get on board," Gene said. "We've got a little bit of business to take care of."

"No problem," Rob answered. "There are drinks and snacks in the galley; feel free to take anything you want."

As they were climbing the stairs to the plane, Paul called up to them, "I'll be up to make some fresh coffee in a couple of minutes if you want."

"That would be great," Gene said as Jim entered the cabin of the Gulfstream IV. "Take your time, there's no rush."

"Anything new?" Jim asked, taking one of the plush leather seats facing rearward after seeing Gene's briefcase in the opposite seat.

"Not much," Gene answered, picking up his briefcase and sitting. "Mainly, our meeting with the Senator. Any subsequent meetings are completely off the record.

As a matter of fact, he is reported to be in Oklahoma meeting with some oil production company," Gene continued. "If there was ever an operation that could never be discovered, this one is at the top of the list."

Opening the briefcase, he pulled out a list of names and handed it to Jim, saying, "Here's the latest. You'll probably notice a couple of additions. But they have no more or no less importance than the others. We will be discussing the order of their elimination in New Orleans.

The final authority will come from IL," Gene emphasized after Jim handed the list back. "If we're lucky, most of the operation will just consist of confronting the individuals and letting them extract themselves from the situation."

"Do you really expect that to work?" Jim asked, thinking about how people at the upper levels of government would react to the threat of exposure.

"That's a complete unknown," Gene answered, shaking his head. "But, given the number of people involved, I hope so. When I was first approached, I asked what would happen if all of these people suddenly disappeared in a relatively short period of time. The answer was basically that would be an unacceptable scenario."

"Where does that leave us?" Jim asked as he heard someone coming up the stairs to the plane.

"Following the guidance I just mentioned," Gene answered as Paul approached them.

"Our coffeemaker is a single service type," Paul said as he reached their seats. "I'll bring you the types, and you can choose."

"Whatever you have that's close to Folgers Original blend is good for me," Jim said, nodding.

"Same here," Gene told him. "No cream or sugar needed. But, any kind of breakfast bar would be greatly appreciated."

"I'll leave you with a basket of what we have," Paul said as he prepared the coffeemaker for the first cup.

After serving both of them and setting the basket of breakfast bars on the seat across the aisle from Gene, Paul said, "I've got to get back to work. If you need anything else, just let me know."

"I'm pretty sure I can work the coffeemaker," Jim said, smiling. "It's about the same as I've used in hotels all over the country."

"And it's only about an hour and a half flight," Gene added. "We can take care of anything we need, but thank you, Paul."

"No problem," Paul said, seeing Rob enter the plane. "But if there's anything …"

"Got it, we'll yell for you," Gene told him reaching for a rice crispy bar with chocolate chips. "We'll see you in New Orleans."

Chapter Fifteen

After landing at the New Orleans Naval Air Station, Joint Reserve Base (NAS/JRB), Rob taxied the Gulfstream to the ramp, where a ground support team awaited their arrival.

As soon as the engines were shut down, Paul lowered the stairs and informed Gene that his transportation to the hotel had just pulled up on the ramp.

Thanking Rob, Gene, and Jim descended the stairs and walked the short distance to where a driver stood holding the rear door open to Gene's preferred vehicle, a black Suburban with blacked-out windows.

As they entered, Gene nodded to another gentleman sitting in the front passenger seat and said, "Jim, this is Michael Powers. He's the lead of the pre-arrival team and will give us a quick brief on the way to the hotel."

"Nice to meet you, Michael," Jim said, leaning forward to shake his hand.

"You, too," Michael replied. "Please, it's just Mike."

Turning to look at Gene, he asked, "Are you ready for the status, sir?"

"Go ahead," Gene said.

"We booked six rooms at the Hilton New Orleans Airport three days ago," Mike told him. "All on the bottom floor at the rear of the hotel, three rooms on each side of the hall adjacent to the rear exit. As you approach the exit, the SCIF was set up in the middle room, number 139, on the right-hand side of the hall. We had it up and operational on the second day and have run continuous checks, all with zero faults.

The other rooms were merely to provide additional buffer areas, and we installed white noise generators in each room in the event someone tried to monitor any conversations outside of the SCIF. All of the internal wiring within and above all six rooms has been tapped, and a buzz will be the only thing possibly heard if someone is attempting to use the electrical system to listen in," he continued.

"Your guest will be arriving in approximately 30 minutes," Mike informed them. "We have a car waiting at Signature Flight Support to bring him to the hotel.

The New Orleans airport is only a few minutes from the hotel, and the team will bring him to the rear exit where the rooms are located," Mike told them as they left the base.

"We're about fifteen minutes from the hotel, so you'll have sufficient time to go over all of our preparations and ask any questions before he gets there," Mike finished. "Do you have any questions?"

"How many members of your team are here?" Jim asked.

"There are eight of us, sir," Mike answered. "Two are at the airport waiting for your guest's airplane to land, and the other four, besides the driver and I, are at the hotel. One of them is in room 139 monitoring all of the electronic signals, two are stationed in the hall, and the final guy is in a van parked just outside the rear exit monitoring the exterior."

"How are you going to deploy your men once Jim and I meet in 139?" Gene asked. "I certainly don't want someone wandering down the hall just as our guest comes in the rear exit."

"Understand," Mike answered, nodding. "The two men that are in the hall outside of the rooms will be split once we arrive. One of them will reposition to the van, and those two will ensure there's no one around the exit when our car arrives. The other will be at the head of the hall and will notify the team if anyone is headed that way. The two men with your guest will escort the guest to the door, and I'll be inside the door to open it if the hall is clear.

We have made several practice runs, and this is the optimum use of the people," Mike added.

"What do you think, Jim?" Gene asked.

"That sounds as good as you can get with the number of men," Jim answered. "And having more men may cause more problems than the slight risk of someone seeing our guest. And even if he's spotted, the odds that he will be recognized are slim. The only thing I can think of to add that wouldn't take much time would be to turn off the hall lights in the area where the rooms are located."

"That's a good idea," Mike said, nodding. "The only lights at that end of the hall are over the doors at each room. I'll have that done before your guest gets to the hotel. And we can have them back on as soon as he leaves."

Gene looked at Jim and, seeing him nod, said, "Well, I guess that's as good as it gets. Unless we throw a blanket over his head as he gets out of the car."

"I'm betting there isn't a blanket in the car," Jim said, shaking his head. "Who's going to go running out of the exit with a blanket to wrap it around someone? Don't you think that might draw just a wee bit of attention?"

"Can you spell facetious?" Gene asked as they pulled into the parking lot of the Hilton. "I'll loan you my Funk and Wagnalls if you need it."

"Nope, don't need it," Jim said as they got out of the car. "I'm just a little surprised that your sense of humor didn't stay back in Texas, given the gravity of this operation. Maybe you are developing a new sense of humor because of it … gallows humor."

Chapter Sixteen

A few minutes after checking the rooms and ensuring every safeguard was working as required, Mike told Gene, "Your guest just left the airport. They expect to be here in eight minutes. I'm going to move my men to their new positions."

"That sounds good," Gene agreed. "Let everyone know to bring him directly to room 139, and I'll receive him. Just make sure the guys outside are watching for any sign of cameras in the distance. And, have the car pull as close to the exit door as possible."

"We're ready," Mike replied, nodding. "Also, the guy bringing the guest had a fake beard and sunglasses with him, and he'll be wearing them."

"Good," Gene told him. "I'll keep the door open until he's inside with Jim and me. Once he's inside with us, I want another electronic sweep for any devices in the room that may have remained dormant. Then make a sweep of the halls and the floor above our room," He looked at Mike. "I'll let you know when we're done, and you can take the guest back to the airport."

"Yes, sir," Mike replied. "I'll go check on my guys and send someone in to sweep the room as you suggested."

A couple of minutes later, Gene heard the exit door opening, and he stepped into the hall. He saw Senator Knowles following Mike and another man. To the left, down the hall, he saw two others blocking the entrance to the lobby area.

As Mike approached, Gene stepped into the hall and greeted the Senator. "Good morning, sir. If you'll just step inside for a moment, we have one last security measure before we get started."

As they entered the room, Mike shut the door, and the man with him began thoroughly sweeping the walls, paying particular attention to the lights' electrical outlets and switch boxes.

Giving his all clear, he and Mike left the room, and Gene led Senator Knowles to the SCIF. As Jim followed them inside and shut the door, Gene said, "This man will be in charge of the daily operations."

As Jim shook his hand, Jackson said, "I've read your bio, young man. But are you sure you want to be involved in this?"

"Sir, I can only say that from what I've read and have been told," Jim answered, nodding to Gene, "I trust both of you that we're doing the right thing. So, yes, I want to be involved."

Jackson nodded and sat across the small table from where Gene stood. "Please, sit."

As Jim and Gene took the chairs across the table from him, Jackson began, "You remember the letter I sent regarding how this endeavor may be viewed, don't you?"

Seeing Jim nod, he continued, "Do you know how many men signed the Declaration of Independence? Fifty-six.

What those fifty-six brave men did mean risking their fortunes, their reputations, and, more importantly, their lives.

I hope you've considered that," Jackson said, looking directly into Jim's eyes.

Turning to Gene, he added, "You, too."

After a pause, Jackson continued, "Now, I'm going to tell you why this must happen. If you then decide you want no part of it, I'll understand, and you'll be free to go. No one except the three of us knows who we are, and no one else will ever know."

Sitting back in his chair, Jackson began, "I'm sure you've seen what's been going on in our country over the last few years. People have been losing faith in our institutions.

I'm speaking of our formerly admired institutions like the CIA, the FBI, and even our local and state police departments," he continued. "And it's not just the government. It's our religious institutions, our educational institutions, those institutions that provide so much of what our forefathers dreamed of when those 56 men risked everything to give us the opportunity to have this once great nation.

That nation is under attack," he said, looking from Jim to Gene. "Under attack from within. We are under attack because we, the people, have let too many seemingly minor deviations from our moral code slip by. Those few are like an infection. Unless treated, it spreads.

And it has spread across our country, infecting those institutions that used to provide us with a feeling of security, of freedom to pursue the things that people worldwide can only dream of," he told them.

"Now, every name you've been given has crossed that line," Jackson said sadly, shaking his head. "It's time to try

to put this train back on path. At least we must try. We owe
that to our future countrymen. I'm proud of my country, as
I'm sure you both are judging from your service up to this
point. If you still want to continue, I'll tell you how I believe
this must be done."

Chapter Seventeen

Seeing both Gene and Jim nod, Jackson told them, "My main goal is to remove those people from positions of power, whether it's the government, one of the established religious organizations, or one of our major corporations. When people believe themselves untouchable, they become tyrannical and flaunt the laws, morals, or codes of conduct that the rest of us must live under.

Now, I don't consider myself other than a normal guy who has been blessed with a chance to do something for my country. This could have been done a million ways, but it seems that no one wants to step up.

I've spoken with my colleagues at length regarding this issue. They almost to the man see the problem but don't want the responsibility to resolve it. If we're not responsible, we, the elected members of our government, then who is?" Jackson asked. "I'll tell you who is responsible; we all are. Not just the elected officials, but the people who elected them.

Now, I can somewhat excuse the electorate because our system is designed to ensure that each of us, me included, gets to return to our office," he told them. "And the *scratch my back and I'll scratch yours* mentality at this level borders on being immoral. When a person knows about a situation, such as we have with the people on the list, and does nothing, he or she is just as guilty."

He paused to let them absorb all of that information. "Now I believe in our system of government, regardless of what I just criticized about the people who elected the people we're discussing, it's still the best form of government I know of.

Having said that, I believe in it; I'm trying to find a way to maintain it as we attempt to purge the filth from the system. That includes the companies who have placed the wrong people in charge, the religious institutions that have allowed the wrong people to oversee their moral education, as well as our elected officials.

So, in my attempt to rid these organizations of those people who have lost their moral compass, I will do my very best to maintain the balance of power, especially within the elected officials, as much as possible until they can be replaced via the ballot box," Jackson explained.

"Currently, the Senate Democrats have a one-seat advantage, as well as the tie-breaking vote, if necessary," he informed them. "Each of the people on the list who hold those positions will be encouraged to seek other employment in a certain order.

Compounding our problem is the method of replacing any outgoing official," Jackson said. "In thirty-seven of the states, the seat is filled by gubernatorial appointment, and then the replacement is voted in on a special election on the next regularly scheduled election, and it may or may not be the appointed person.

In the other thirteen states, a special election is required within a certain amount of time," he continued. "I'm going to do my best to ensure that if a blue party member resigns, then I'll wait until he or she is replaced before I continue.

I'm guessing that if the Governor of the state is blue, he will appoint blue," the Senator continued. "If he doesn't, then I may change my priorities. As I stated at the beginning, I believe in our form of government. The people elect the officials. At least at some point in the thirty-seven states I first discussed.

I want the people to make the decision in an election. If the special election changes an outgoing blue to a red, that's their decision," he explained. "I'm not going to stop the balance of power from shifting if it's the will of the people.

I'm just not going to try to reverse it by removing all the blue before the red," he added. "That's why the order for any action regarding the people on the list comes from me. Since several of the people I have noted are up for reelection next year, I'll direct how they will be offered an escape route.

I hope there will not be any violence necessary," Jackson told them. "These are intelligent people. I'm hoping that just knowing they will be exposed if they don't leave office will result in our desired outcome. But, as my great-great-grandfather always said, "Some people are just plain stupid, *and that will never change."* I have high hopes that those are few and can be convinced that the only path forward is to resign."

Chapter Eighteen

"What about for the House of Representatives?" Jim asked. "There are more people on the list from the House than the Senate."

"Vacancies in the House are filled by special election," Jackson answered. "That process differs depending on whether it's during the first session of Congress or the second.

It's up to the *Executive Authority*, meaning the Governor of the state," Jackson continued. "They may try to schedule it to coincide with an election of local issues in the district affected by the vacancy. Or they may hold a special election just for that seat.

Members of the House of Representatives have two-year terms, and approximately one-third of the total seats are up for election every year," Jackson said. "Even though there are more on the list, the ratio is approximately the same, roughly seven percent.

My biggest concern with this is the length of time it may take to complete our mission," he added. "This could take up to two years to fill the vacancies.

I'm hoping that we can accelerate that somewhat, but it would be very strange to have 32 congressmen leave office within a couple of months," he continued. "I want this completed within six months. The vacancies may not be filled, especially in the House, but I want those people out of office within that time frame."

"What about the religious issue?" Jim asked, thinking about the Baptist preacher.

"Time-wise, I'm not concerned," the Senator answered. "By the way, it's not just one. But I'm having the others taken care of by a close friend in that field.

The same goes for the folks in the civilian corporate world," he continued. "I'm not too concerned about the time involved. Corporations have established methods of replacing outgoing Chief Executive Officers or other upper management personnel.

We'll approach the person involved and let them decide their fate," Jackson finished. "I'm pretty sure that once they know what lies in store, they'll want to save their retirement plan and avoid a most embarrassing situation."

"Not to doubt your ability to gain me access to these individuals, but I would see that as a major issue," Jim told him. "Especially since you don't want your name involved, nor do I want mine. And I'll bet my friend here doesn't either."

"A secure message will be sent," Jackson told him. "It will be from an unknown source from an unidentifiable server. The message will only ask for an appointment for an individual to have a closed-door meeting.

The message will be from a *well-established children's charity organization,*" Jackson continued, giving air quotes. "It's called *The Children of El Barco*. I feel sure that will open any doors with no names needing to be given.

And I'm also sure that you'll come up with an appropriate name for yourself," Jackson said, grinning. "I'd recommend having business cards printed with *The Children of El Barco* and your pseudo name and a phone number from some South American country. Brazil comes to mind."

"We're already working on that," Gene told him. "Our sister operations are underway and will fit nicely with this. That is if we can get started within the next couple of weeks."

"Good," Jackson said. "I'll have the first name for you tomorrow. And with most things, it's best to work from the top down."

Jim sat stunned for a moment before asking, "Are you directing me to approach …"

"Somebody has to," the Senator answered, standing. "Just remember, he works for you. Think of it as your gardener who got caught in bed with your wife. Would you fire him?"

Jim rose and answered, "No doubt. Then I'd fire the wife."

Jackson laughed and said, "I'll bet it's easier to find a good gardener, though. Maybe you'll be lucky enough to find a good wife that wants to garden. Now, if you gentlemen have no further questions or suggestions, I've got to get back to my job before I'm fired."

Chapter Nineteen

As they headed back to the base for the flight home, Jim asked, "What are the preparations that have been made regarding the messages about *The Children of El Barco*?"

"We established the organization and had it inserted into an international list of recognized charities," Gene answered. "Anyone looking into it will find it was established over 50 years ago to help refugee children return to their families in their country of origin if anything happens to their parents here in the States or anywhere else in the world. Requests for your audience with the selected individual will be on their letterhead and will be sent from the Brazilian Embassy here in the US. We have contacted the Ambassador and explained that embassy assistance would be greatly appreciated."

"Do you think that will be enough to gain access to these people, especially the top ones?" Jim asked.

"I'm pretty sure just the name of the yacht, with a reference to children, will open doors," Gene answered, nodding. "Now, I know we'll have to jump through some hoops, especially with the first one. But I'm betting that he'll figure out a way to find out what you, or the Children of the Boat, know and, more importantly, want.

And I'm just as sure that he'll want to find a way to silence you," Gene told him earnestly. "I wouldn't put it past him or his people to take some very aggressive steps to prevent you from releasing the information."

"What information, or proof of his involvement, do we have?" Jim asked as they approached the base.

"We, that is, Dark Water, infiltrated the Brazilian side of the operation over a year ago when we first learned of how many of our political or other leaders were involved," Gene answered.

"We also have people in Honolulu who are part of the ground crew that takes care of the yacht when it's in port," he continued. "They have been installing cameras throughout the yacht as well as listening devices that can be activated from Black Water headquarters when we want to monitor their time at sea."

"I think I see Bracer's hand in this," Jim replied, knowing how the company could insert itself into anyone's life. "I'm guessing the company also has infected the phones with their special software."

"Pretty much," Gene agreed. "But we don't have access to the offices of our first target. And, 1 don't think it would do any good anyway. I really doubt if you'll get any admission from him in any meeting.

I've discussed that particular issue and how best to approach him," Gene continued. "We think that the best approach is to let him know we have the information and will not use it if he decides not to run for reelection. He has about eighteen months left in office, and this will give him a chance to leave without the disgrace of having his reputation smeared across the world."

"Do you actually think he'll come after me?" Jim asked. "I mean, he has every asset of the government at his disposal. If he truly wanted to silence me, it wouldn't be too difficult."

"We've thought of that," Gene told him. "For this special visit, you'll be disguised as a priest from Brazil, and you'll be accompanied by Sister Margarita from the Children's organization.

All documents provided regarding your visit will show you in black robes, a beard, glasses, some modifications to your cheekbones, and white gloves should you touch anything," Gene explained.

"Sister Margarita will be disguised as well," Gene added. "The people at Quantico have taken hundreds of pictures of you and the Sister and photo-shopped them to find the most effective means of hiding any single item that could be used to identify either of you."

"Who is *Sister Margarita*?" Jim asked as they entered the flight line where their Gulfstream was waiting.

"An old acquaintance," Gene answered as they pulled beside the plane. "She worked with you back in Atlanta, even though you didn't know it at the time."

"Jewell," Jim said, nodding. "Why her?"

"First, she's fluent in Portuguese," Gene answered as Rob came down from the plane to meet them. "And, she hasn't been active for enough time for anyone to remember her. Sort of like getting an unknown face, but with years of experience."

"Is she going to be involved with all of the operations?" Jim asked as they boarded the plane.

"Nope," Gene answered as they headed for their seats. "She'll disappear after your first audience with the target. We don't want to put her in the crosshairs of any efforts to silence you."

"But you'll leave me with a laser dot on my forehead," Jim remarked as they took their seats.

"I have faith in you," Gene told him, smiling as he sat down.

Chapter Twenty

Three days later, Jim arrived back at DFW after finishing his trip, and as he rode the small tram that carried airport employees back and forth to the parking lot, he started wondering when Gene would request him to head to Quantico.

Within minutes of walking in his door, his phone rang. Expecting it to be Marie, he answered by saying, "Miss me?"

"Desperately," Gene answered, laughing. "But I doubt if you're too concerned about me missing you. Maybe Marie, but definitely not me."

"That's for sure," Jim replied, laughing. "But it's always good to hear from you, too. Now, tell me you've decided to call off this entire mission of morals we've become embroiled in."

"Not at all," Gene answered. "But that is the reason for the call. I'll be at Love Field at nine o'clock tomorrow morning, and we'll head to Chicago to pick up Jewell. Then we'll fly to Quantico."

"I just barely got home," Jim argued. "Couldn't this wait until I've had a day off?"

"Can't," Gene replied. "We need to get you and Jewell to Quantico and have the makeup people do their stuff so we can get the pictures we need. Our friend in Washington is chomping at the bit to get the operation rolling. He's drafted letters for each of the people on the lists and wants to fire the first shot as soon as we can.

To set up the first meeting, we need to make sure you and Jewell are unidentifiable. I'm sure once the *request* for a meeting is delivered, they'll run your photographs through every facial recognition program available to try to identify either or both of you.

That's why this first session is one of the most important," Gene told him. "Once the makeup people are finished, we'll run the photos through our own version of facial recognition and look for any flaws."

"How long will we be gone?" Jim asked as he started unpacking his suitcase.

"With any luck at all, I'll have you home late tomorrow evening," Gene answered. "But, no later than noon the next day."

"I'll pack for three days," Jim replied, pulling the dirty clothes from his trip from the suitcase. "Somehow, every time you take me to Quantico for a day, it turns into two or three. And I'm guessing this will be the same."

"I'm hoping not," Gene countered. "The team has had hundreds of pictures of you and Jewell and photoshopped them hundreds of ways.

Then they ran them through the same recognition programs to see what features they need to adjust," Gene explained. "Then they developed what was unrecognizable to any of the programs and gave those photos to the makeup folks. Using some sort of computer program, they constructed mannequin heads of both of you and figured out how to transform them into the faces in the pictures. That should make the actual process much faster since they know where to start and what the end result should be."

"I hope you're right," Jim said, tossing clean underwear and socks into the suitcase. "I'd hate to have either the picture you send or one of the hundreds of photos I'm sure will be taken at used to identify either me or Jewell."

"That's one reason why she'll only be used once," Gene told him. "And we're making an assumption that if your disguise works the first time, it'll be good for the next time."

"Have you given any thought to what the first meeting will produce as a way of threats?" Jim asked, putting a clean pair of jeans and two T-shirts in the suitcase.

"Of course," Gene answered. "We figure he'll have a team watching the meeting place for at least 24 hours before the meeting. And we figure he'll have another team ready to follow you after the meeting is concluded.

For now, we're concentrating on making sure you can't be identified," Gene explained. "We'll have our own people watching and we don't believe anything will happen until our guest has left the scene.

Our two biggest windows of threat are when you are there waiting and when you are leaving," Gene continued. "We don't think it will be before he arrives because he'll want to know what you know and your demands. That places our primary concern on the time from when he leaves and when you leave. Even though he has been at that location numerous times, we can't assume that his security will be the least bit lax, so we're rather limited in what we can have in place prior to his arrival."

"Okay," Jim told him. "Guess I'm in your hands, and I really hope that those makeup folks know their business. I'd hate to have my face fall off like it did in that scene from

Mrs. Doubtfire when she was giving that guy the Heimlich maneuver."

"I'm sure your face won't fall off," Gene said, laughing. "But I'm going to have our people game the entire scenario from your arrival to departure to find any way to get you out of the area. I still concentrate on your vulnerability after he leaves, but nothing's off the table."

"I agree with that premise," Jim replied. "At least that's when I'd try if I did anything. The big unknown is what he'll think he can do if he feels threatened. Or, if he'll wait for the other shoe to drop before taking any action."

"I'm sure you're right," Gene agreed. "But, sometimes, people that are threatened want to lash out at the messenger before considering the consequences. Remember, he'll know we still have copies of the information that he's going to be looking at. And he'll have to realize that it may just be the tip of the iceberg. There are lots of reasons he'll want to wait to see what could be next."

"And all he'll know he can do at this point is try to capture either Jewell or me," Jim told him. "I'd make that my top priority."

"We're planning on that being their priority also," Gene replied. "And we're working on contingency plans. Anyway, I'll have more for you tomorrow, and you'll get a briefing from the team that will be in place during the operation."

"Okay, I'll see you tomorrow morning," Jim told him. "Will you at least have breakfast on the plane for me?"

"Sure," Gene said, laughing. "We've contracted with Denny's to cater to every flight you're on."

Chapter Twenty-One

The following morning, Jim was waiting at Love Field when Gene's plane taxied up to the General Aviation terminal. As the ground personnel parked the Gulfstream and a fuel truck pulled in front of the right-wing, Jim walked out carrying his suitcase.

Once the engines were shut down, the stairs were lowered, and Gene came down with the Captain to meet him.

"How was the flight?" Jim asked, shaking Gene's hand.

"Normal," Gene answered. "This is Captain Ronny Jackson. He'll be taking us all the way to Quantico."

"Good to meet you, Captain," Jim said, shaking his hand. "Gonna be a long day."

"Normal for me," he replied. "Just call me Ronny. Mike is the copilot and will be flying the leg to Chicago. Go ahead and get on board. I've just got to recheck the weather and make sure the flight plan is ready as soon as we're refueled."

"Anything new?" Jim asked as he followed Gene up the stairs.

"Not really," Gene answered as they headed for their seats. "The makeup people have finally decided on what needs to be done. This will be more or less a dress rehearsal to make sure the photos are unidentifiable as you."

"Any word from our client, IL?" Jim asked, taking the rear-facing seat across the small table from Gene.

"No," Gene answered, pulling a sheet of paper from his briefcase. "Just a little rearranging of the sequencing."

"How's Jewell's role coming along?" Jim asked, taking the sheet from Gene.

"She's not playing much of a role," Gene answered. "She's been given a script in the event our man starts asking her questions. But I have confidence she can ad-lib when necessary."

"How long from when the pictures are approved, and the letter of *introduction* will be sent?" Jim asked as the copilot came back toward them.

"Probably the next day," Gene answered.

"You must be Jim," the copilot said as Jim stood.

"Yes, sir, that would be me," Jim replied, shaking his hand. "And you must be Mike."

"That I am," he answered. "This is the Captain's leg, so I'll be the guy you'll call if you need anything in flight."

Jim looked at Gene and asked, "Did Denny's get my breakfast order on board, or are we going to have to wait?"

Mike looked at Gene and asked, "Are we expecting catering?"

"No," Gene answered, laughing. "Jim has this obsession with Denny's. We'll make do with the normal stuff you have on board."

"Now I'm disappointed," Jim replied, shaking his head. "I was really hoping for a Grand Slam."

"Well, guess you'll have to wait until we get to Quantico," Mike told him. "But, if there's anything else, I'll try accommodating you."

"I'll be fine," Jim said, smiling. "I've got to give the General a hard time whenever I get a chance."

"I understand," Mike replied.

"Now, is there anything I can get you before we takeoff?"

"No thanks," Jim answered. "I've had all the coffee I can take, and I'm sure I can find the galley if I need anything."

"Okay," Mike said, turning to go back to the cockpit. "Just yell if you need help,"

"Have you gotten a copy of the letter or the script for me?" Jim asked, taking his seat.

"Just so happens that I do," Gene answered, pulling some other papers from his briefcase. "Just read through these once we get going, and let me know if you have any comments."

As Jim glanced at the pages, Ronny came onboard and told them that everything was ready and they'd be taxing out as soon as the fuel truck was out of the way.

As he entered the cockpit, Jim asked, "What's the plan if we don't get an audience?"

"So far, none that I know of," Gene answered. "But the consensus is that he'll make sure it happens."

"If he doesn't, we've wasted a lot of time and money," Jim replied as they heard the first engine being started. "And we will have made some very powerful enemies if he decides to be proactive."

"We're going to make some very powerful enemies regardless," Gene told him as the plane began to move forward. "Very powerful."

Chapter Twenty-Two

After landing at Midway International Airport in Chicago, Jim returned the sheets back to Gene and asked, "Does Jewell need to know what's in these papers?"

"I believe so," Gene answered, putting them in his briefcase. "I think she kind of needs to know the basics, but I'm depending on you to keep things on track regarding the conversation. By that, I mean ensuring that he understands just how damning the evidence is. The problem with people in his position is they think they can control any situation just because of their position. And that includes CEO's or leaders of any organization."

"Looks like Jewell's ready to go to work," Jim remarked, seeing her leave the building a short distance from where they had parked.

"She's been asking for an assignment for the last couple of years," Gene told him as they watched her sprint across the tarmac.

"I'll be right back," Mike told them as he headed for the stairs. "I'll get any luggage the lady left inside while I check on the weather and flight plan."

No sooner had he left the plane when Jewell came rushing into the cabin, saying, "It's about time. How long has it been? Three years? Four?"

"I don't remember," Jim answered, standing to accept her energetic hug. "Been quite a while."

Jewell stepped back and said, "I'm so sorry about Jennifer. And I know what it's like trying to recover from what happened to you."

"I'm sure you do," Jim said, smiling. "All those years after the crash, trying to regain your life. You've been through a lot."

"Gene, it's good to see you again also," she said, giving him a quick hug. "Thank you for the chance to get back to work. I've missed it."

"I'm just glad that you've made such a remarkable recovery," he replied, returning her hug. "Now, I'm going to leave you two together for a couple of minutes while I go inside to check on how things are going at Quantico."

As he left the plane, Jewell turned to Jim and said, "I think he just wanted for us to have a few minutes alone."

"Probably," Jim agreed. "I think he's a little worried about our working together again after all that's happened. Especially since this is not the ordinary operation we're used to."

"I've thought about this for some time," Jewell said, taking a seat across the aisle from where Gene and Jim had been sitting. "I must admit, I've also been just a little apprehensive."

Jim took his seat and said, "I understand. But I don't expect any issues between us. The past is just that … the past. I hope you understand that as well."

"Yeah, I know," Jewell said, looking into Jim's eyes sadly. "As I said earlier, I'm sorry about Jennifer, and I understand you've met someone who makes you happy."

"Yes, Marie is a terrific lady," Jim told her as Mike entered the plane with a small suitcase. "I'm a lucky guy to meet someone like her. What about you?"

"Still holding out hope," she answered as she watched Mike set her suitcase in the baggage area at the front of the plane. "But, one day at a time."

"You guys need anything?" Mike asked, walking toward them.

"Nothing for me," Jim answered.

"Me neither," Jewell told him. "But, thanks for asking." As Mike got into the cockpit, Gene returned to where they were sitting and said, "Everything is ready at Quantico. If we can get the makeup folks done and the photos taken as they expect, we'll have you guys home tomorrow morning."

"When do you expect us to make the first contact?" Jewell asked as Gene took his seat.

"If the photos are done, the letter will go out tomorrow as well," Gene told her, opening his briefcase. "Then it's up to the target to set the meeting. But we're pushing for less than a week.

You need to take a look at how we're framing the scenario," he continued, handing her the same sheets Jim had looked at. "Now, just keep in mind that this is the basic framework. Jim will have to adjust the conversation if it seems to be getting off course. Your job is mainly to be there to add authenticity and support Jim."

"Do you really think he'll believe we're just members of the *Children of the Boat*?" she asked, glancing at the papers.

"Not once he sees the evidence you'll provide him," Gene answered. "That's when it becomes important to have two of you there. Just another deterrent against any action happening at the meeting. We'll get more into that on the flight home tomorrow. For now, just get a feel for how we envision the operation to unfold."

Chapter Twenty-Three

After landing at Quantico and arriving at Black Water Headquarters, Jim and Jewell were escorted to the room where they met with the people who were going to transform their appearance to prevent facial recognition programs from identifying them.

As Jim sat in the chair staring at a bust of his face on the table in front of him, he remarked, "If you hadn't told me that was my head, I'd never have believed it. And I've been looking at my face for several years."

"That's the point," the makeup artist responded as he took several latex patches from a tray. "I'm Taylor, and I'll be trying to match you to the bust.

The biggest thing we had to do was to change the shape of your nose. You have a typical American Indian nose," he continued as he swabbed the sides of Jim's nose with alcohol pads. "A prominent hump in the center and rather narrow."

Taking a small piece of the latex, he placed it on one side of Jim's nose and said, "This will add some depth to the sides of the nose and make it appear flatter than it is. Once I get both sides done, I'll use some colored makeup to blend it into your face."

Finishing that, he took another piece of latex and added it to an area just above Jim's cheekbones and told him, "This will reduce the prominence of your cheekbones and make your face appear slightly wider.

Then, when I apply the bushier eyebrows and the beard, you'll look exactly like the bust in front of you," Taylor continued.

A couple of minutes later, he held a mirror up to let Jim see the transformation, asking, "What do you think?"

"Who the hell is that guy?" Jim joked, turning his head to look at his new face from different angles. "I don't think I know him."

"Just wait until we get the wig, colored contact lenses, and glasses," Taylor told him, setting the mirror on the table. "But first, we'll take several shots from every angle and see what the computer says."

Jim sat quietly as two men with cameras walked around him and photographed him from the sides, below, and above, trying to get every feature of his head and face.

Once they had finished, Taylor came over and asked Jim to follow him into an adjoining room. "Here's the costume you'll be wearing," he said, pointing to a stand with a purple Cassock and a gold rope tied around the waist.

"And this will be your hat," he told Jim, holding up a black Biretta with bright red stripes and a ball on top.

"Let's go ahead and start getting dressed while we wait for the final verdict from the computer folks," he said, taking the Cassock off the stand. "Just put your clothes on the table here, and we'll get started."

"Are you going to take more pictures of me dressed to see if it changes my recognition?" Jim asked as he pulled off his boots.

"Of course," Taylor said, untying the rope around the Cassock. "But the main things the recognition program looks at aren't the clothes. It's bone structure, like the shape of your chin, or the distance between your eyes, or the distance from your nose to your mouth.

Since clothes can be changed easily, mustaches can be shaved or grown; hair can be cut or grown longer, they don't really change the recognition," he continued as Jim finished undressing.

"Here, put this on," Taylor said, holding out the Cassock. "We used your measurements to make sure it would fit. And just pull the rope snug around your waist."

As Jim slipped the Cassock over his head, Taylor pointed to a pair of black round-toed leather slippers with purple trim, saying, "These will be your shoes. Not quite like the boots you just took off but more in keeping with the religious appearance we're shooting for."

As Jim pulled on the slippers, Bracer came into the room smiling and asked, "Just who the hell are you, Mister?"

"Bracer, so nice to see you again," Jim said, straightening up. "I assume you're overseeing this little charade as far as the facial recognition stuff."

"That I am," she said, shaking Jim's hand. "I'm going to brag a little and say that the program I've developed is far superior to anything else out there. If you can fool my program, you'll definitely fool any of the others.

And, I just finished running your new and *greatly* improved, I must say, face through the program, and it came up with ten possible matches," she informed him.

"I hope those ten people don't include me," Jim replied as Taylor handed him the wig.

"Nope," Bracer answered as Jim put on the wig. "We ran each photo of you before and after to see the number of points that might appear the same, and it was zero.

That's about as good as it gets," she continued as Taylor sat the Biretta on Jim's head.

"So, I guess we'll finish dressing and shoot the pictures again?" Jim asked after putting in the dark brown contact lens and the black-rimmed glasses on.

"Of course," Bracer answered. "But I don't expect any changes regarding recognition. We'll probably just use the photos for the operation."

"What about Jewell?" Jim asked, looking in the mirror.

"Another perfect zero," she answered as Taylor made some minor adjustments to the Cassock. "Now, we'll head over to have your glamour shots taken."

Chapter Twenty-Four

The next morning, after having breakfast in the Black Water cafeteria, Gene escorted Jim and Jewell back to where the airplane was parked.

As they arrived, he wished them a quick, safe trip and advised them that the first request for a meeting would be delivered by noon.

"While you're waiting for further information," he told them, walking with them to the stairs of the plane, "just think about what could happen if this all goes terribly wrong.

You can still opt out if that's what you believe is best for you," he said as they watched the flight crew coming their way. "If I haven't heard from you by the time we get a response from the first person, I'll assume you're prepared to proceed.

Now, if there are any changes or further information, I'll contact you," he finished as the flight crew stopped at the foot of the stairs where they were standing.

"Good morning," the man with the four stripes denoting a Captain said. "I'm Troy Baker, and this is Frank Purser, my copilot. We'll be taking you back to Chicago Midway and Love Field if that's correct."

"That's correct," Gene said, nodding. "If there are any problems, have ops give me a call."

"I don't foresee any problems," Troy told him. "The weather for both legs is clear, and reports of smooth air. While Frank checks the exterior, I'll be glad to help you get settled and answer any questions."

Jim looked at Jewell and then said, "We were both on this plane yesterday, and I appreciate your offer, but I don't think we'll need anything."

"You're not going to ask him about the catering by Denny's?" Gene asked, smiling.

As Troy started to say something with a quizzical look on his face, Jim answered, "No. If you'll remember, we just finished breakfast. Let's try not to bother the Captain with unnecessary issues."

Gene shook his head and told Troy, "Old private joke, Captain. Just ignore these two and have a safe flight."

Turning to give Jewell a quick hug, he told her, "Good to have you back. But, if you …"

"Not to worry, sir," she replied. "I'm not backing out. I've waited too long for a chance to get another operational mission. I've been sidelined long enough."

"Same for me," Jim said, shaking Gene's hand. "Just say the word, and we'll be ready."

"You know you've only got two more days off before you go back to work," Gene told him. "I don't expect any action that soon, but it could happen. If there are any conflicts with American Airlines, I'm sure they can be worked out."

"I'm sure you'll find a way," Jim replied. "That wouldn't be the first time my schedule suddenly changed to have another pilot need my flight for '*training*' purposes."

"I'm not sure what you're talking about," Gene said, winking at Jewell. "Neither the company nor I would attempt to interfere with an airline's crew scheduling."

Minutes later, Jim and Jewell were sitting across the aisle from each other, and Jim asked, "Are you comfortable with this operation? I'm not sure if you got the same letter I got regarding treason or sedition, but this is more than just a jab in the leg for someone like in Atlanta."

"I got the same note," Jewell answered as they heard the engines start. "Same answer."

Chapter Twenty-Five

The Gulfstream had barely leveled off after dropping Jewell at Midway when Jim noticed a sharp turn back to the north.

Moments later, Frank stepped from the cockpit and said, "Mr. Lashley, we've just received word from our dispatch that we're to return to Midway and wait for Jewell to return to the airport."

"What's going on?" Jim asked, wondering why they were going back and waiting for Jewell.

"I don't know, sir," Frank answered. "But the company requests that you contact General Barker when we land."

Several minutes later after landing, they taxied to where they had been when Jewell got off and headed home. Jim left the airplane and headed for the operations office to see what had happened.

"General," Jim said as Gene answered his phone. "What's going on?"

"Things got accelerated faster than anticipated," Gene answered. "We had contact with our guy less than an hour after sending him the request for a meeting. It's set for two o'clock tomorrow afternoon at an ice cream parlor he selected."

"What's our plan now?" Jim asked, wondering how they were going to manage such a dramatic acceleration in the timeline.

"I'll brief you and Jewell when you get back here," Gene told him. "You'll both be staying the night here at Quantico in Black Water's facilities. I'll let you know what we're doing to prepare for the meeting and a couple of other issues when you're both here."

"Okay," Jim said. "I guess this is better than getting home and having to come back immediately. Do you think I'll be able to head home after the meeting tomorrow?"

"We'll have to wait and see how it goes," Gene told him. "There are a couple of issues, as I said, that could have an impact. Let's not get ahead of ourselves and just concentrate on the operation at hand."

"Understood," Jim said as he saw Jewell enter the lobby. "By the way, Jewell just walked in, so I guess we'll see you in a couple of hours."

"What's going on?" Jewell asked as she stopped in front of Jim as he was hanging up the phone.

"Our meeting with the gentleman from Washington has been rescheduled to tomorrow afternoon," Jim answered as he looked to make sure no one could overhear them.

"Isn't that sort of unusual?" she asked as they headed back to the plane.

"I don't know, but I'm surprised that he was able to clear his schedule that quickly," Jim answered. "But maybe he didn't have any appointments tomorrow anyway."

"We'll be ready to go when you're both on board," Troy said as they arrived at the stairs leading into the airplane.

"No refueling?" Jim asked, following Jewell up the stairs.

"Not necessary," Troy told him as they entered. "We have more than enough fuel since this is a shorter flight than going to Texas would have been. You guys just find your seats, and we'll be in Virginia as fast as we can make it."

"Is there anything else you haven't told me?" Jewell asked after they were headed east.

"Not really," Jim answered. "Gene said there were a couple of issues but didn't say any more about it other than he'd brief us when we get back to Quantico."

"Any ideas what that's about?" she asked.

"Not a clue," Jim replied. "Possibly, the company has received some additional information that may impact our meeting, but we'll just have to wait until we see Gene."

Chapter Twenty-Six

Gene was waiting for them when they arrived at the terminal at Quantico and took them directly to the Black Water facilities.

Once through the gates and into the main building for Black Water Headquarters, they were taken to their rooms and then met back in the cafeteria.

"Okay, guys, here's what we know," Gene started relating what had happened over the last four hours. "Our man called the number on the letter of introduction about 20 minutes after it was delivered. That's not so unusual, but the biggest thing was from where he made the call. He used a phone that wasn't in his office. Or anywhere in the White House.

Once the meeting was arranged, he then made another call from the same phone to his son, Harry," Gene said. "We've had a bug on Harry's phone for quite some time, so we were able to listen to the conversation.

Now, here's a new factor that you need to consider before the meeting," Gene told them. "After speaking with his father, Harry made a couple of calls and arranged for a team to be at the ice cream parlor waiting for you to leave."

"What are their intentions?" Jim asked. "Surely they don't think that we'd not expect something and have some sort of backup plan."

"My guess is that they intend on holding you hostage until the President comes to some agreement with the *Children of the Boat* folks," Gene replied. "I'm sure Harry's father doesn't want to make any move against you until he's sure of your position. But that won't stop him from *detaining* you until he knows what he's dealing with." Gene looked serious, almost concerned. "But that's not to say Harry won't overreact. He's prone to some rather erratic decisions when faced with an adverse situation."

"What are our plans if there is a team trying to kidnap us?" Jewell asked.

"First, we're monitoring all of the people involved in the initial outreach," Gene assured her. "And we plan on having our own people around the parlor ahead of the meeting, and they'll be there to ensure your safe departure.

Additionally, you'll both be wearing vests beneath your robes that will stop anything short of a 45-caliber bullet," he added. "Also, there will be a Glock 17 9mm pistol taped beneath the table where you'll be meeting with the President."

"Why don't we just carry one each?" Jewell asked.

"In case you're swept for weapons," Gene answered. "It's probably not going to happen, but if you had one and it was discovered, we'd lose control of the situation."

"I agree," Jim said, nodding. "Possibly having one on our person could cause his security team to react, and that would give them a reason to remove us … permanently. We need to be the most benign folks they've ever encountered.

Speaking of the encounter, how's that going to work?" Jim asked.

"You'll both be at the parlor waiting at a table just off the door and beside a large picture window facing onto the street," Gene answered. "You'll both be on the far side of the table with an envelope on the table by the chair across from where you'll be sitting.

We anticipate one of the Secret Service guys to enter and look around before they let the President enter," he continued. "Once he comes in and spots you, you'll rise to acknowledge him and wait for him to approach you.

He'll probably expect some sort of introduction, but he may just take a seat," Gene finished. "You'll have to play that by ear. Just be respectful and make sure he knows that you're only there as messengers."

"Who will I be?" Jim asked, envisioning the meeting.

"You'll be Father Guido Sarducci," Gene told him as he stood. "And Jewell will be Sister Margarita de la Agave. For now, you both need to head to your rooms and try to get some sleep. We'll reconvene tomorrow morning at seven o'clock for breakfast and then head to the makeup area.

I'm sure you'll have more questions in the morning, just as I'm sure we'll have more information," he told them as he escorted them back to their rooms. "But let us worry about making sure things will be handled with your safety and well-being in mind."

Chapter Twenty-Seven

The next morning, after breakfast, Gene escorted Jim and Jewell to the room where they had been when the makeup people had developed their new appearances.

"We had a team watching the parlor all night," Gene told them as a lady started applying Jim's makeup. "There were no suspicious vehicles or people in the surrounding area.

This morning, when the parlor opened, a couple of our agents went in and took the table where you'll be sitting," he continued as he watched Jewell's costume being fitted over the bulletproof vest.

"After they got their ice cream, the guy who was in the chair you'll be using attached your Glock 17 beneath the table where it will be just in front of your right knee," he continued. "If you need it, just slide your hand beneath the table, and you'll find the handle pointing down, ready to grab. And it's loaded with nine rounds of G2 RIP.

We're hoping that you don't have to use it," he added. "But you need to get the gun when you're ready to leave anyway. We expect them to ask you to remain in your seats until the President is back in his car and gone. They might possibly have an agent remain behind to ensure you do, but that's not a problem since he'll be leaving soon after the President's car is gone."

"Have you heard anything further about a possible kidnapping plan?" Jim asked as the last of the makeup was applied to the latex pieces around his nose.

"The four-man team was directed to be in place an hour before the President arrives, so they will be there by one o'clock," Gene answered. "We know they will be driving a black panel van with no windows. The side door slides back, and they will probably be waiting around the corner from the parlor so they can see when to come to the front.

We'll be parked behind the van once we discover where it is," Gene informed them. "We have a double cab, one ton dually, GMC, with a heavy cattle guard in front and four-wheel drive that can shove the van down the street if they stop at the front door as we expect.

Our three agents, besides the driver, can exit quickly and allow you and Jewell to get inside. The agents will jump on the sideboards and keep guard as the truck backs away," Gene explained. "That will be a total of four shooters, not counting the driver, that can counter any attack from the people in the van."

"Do we have anyone in the parlor?" Jim asked as his wig was attached and adjusted.

"No. We thought about that but decided that it would be best to keep the parlor as neutral as possible," Gene answered. "A strange person behind the counter might set off warning bells, and we don't want that. I don't believe we need any additional personnel based on the simulations we ran last night."

"Why don't you give me a gun?" Jewell asked as her headdress was fitted.

"When was the last time you were at the range?" Gene asked. "When was the last time you fired a weapon?"

Gene paused, waiting for her answer, and then said, "I thought so. No, you don't need to become a problem if shooting starts. As we discussed, your role is more to relax the opposition. The presence of a Nun will do that.

And the fact that Jim is portraying a priest, we don't anticipate either of you becoming involved with the actual shooting," Gene added. "But we do need to remove the pistol from the parlor. That is why Jim will be armed when you leave."

"When will we be headed there?" Jim asked as he stood looking at his reflection in the full-length mirror.

"In about an hour," Gene answered as the sash around Jim's robe was adjusted. "So, if either of you need to use the restroom, do it now so we can make any adjustments before we leave. We'll have you there, and you'll be seated in the parlor about thirty minutes before the meeting." Gene admired how well both Jim and Jewell had been transformed.

"Where are the pictures?" Jim asked as the Biretta was placed on top of the wig.

"You'll get them in the car on the way," Gene told him as Jewell came to stand beside Jim. "Do you think you need to see them for any particular reason?"

"Just so I'm familiar with them," Jim answered. "I don't want him to shove one over to me and me not having seen it before.

Believe me, I don't want to see what that pedophile did with those kids. But I want to be able to keep a calm exterior when I'm looking at the photos, if necessary," Jim said as he took a final look at himself and Jewell before they left. "And

I guess I'll have to do it again and again when we go after the other perverts."

"Okay, we have one final check before we leave," Gene told them, handing Jim a phone and earbuds for both. "The phone is connected so both of you can hear what the communication team is saying. Both have microphones, so we can hear anything said within about twenty feet.

The team that's going to bring you back is also tied into the communication network, which is being monitored by Bracer's team," he continued. "For now, let's get a voice check … Jim?"

"Check, one, two, three," Jim said, looking at Jewell.

"One, two, three," Jewell repeated.

"Got it, now how do you hear me?" a voice said into their ears.

"Loud and clear," Jim answered.

"Me, too," Jewell parroted.

"Great," Gene said, heading for the door. "Now, let's get this rolling. Comm, let me know when the other players have checked in and are in position."

Chapter Twenty-Eight

As the black Suburban stopped in front of the small ice cream parlor in Falls Church, Virginia, about nine miles from the Oval Office, Jim checked his Biretta and wig before opening the door.

Holding it open as Jewell stepped out, he looked up and down the street to see if he could spot anything out of the ordinary. Seeing nothing that stood out, he shut the car door and walked to the entrance to the ice cream parlor.

Entering, he saw the table where he had been briefed to sit and then nodded to the man behind the counter as he pulled a chair out for Jewell.

As the man approached them and handed Jim a menu, he asked if they wanted anything to drink.

"Not now, thanks," Jim said, handing the menu to Jewell and pulling out his chair. "We're waiting for someone to join us. We'll let you know when we're ready."

Jim slipped into the chair and pulled up to the table as the man walked away. Sliding his hand down his right leg, he found the handle of the Glock 17 just an inch in front of his knee and slightly to the right.

Satisfied that everything was going as planned so far, he placed the envelope across the table to the chair directly in front of him.

A few minutes later, he heard a lady's voice saying that two vehicles, both appearing to belong to the Secret Service, were leaving the White House.

"Looks like he's on his way," Jim heard in his earpiece. "Expect his arrival in twenty minutes."

"How's my rescue team?" Jim asked quietly as he looked at the menu.

"They're in place," Gene answered. "And they've spotted the van we believe contains the team Harry brought in."

"Anything else I need to know?" Jim said, handing the menu to Jewell.

"It may not mean anything," Gene answered. "But we've heard nothing from any of the opposition players since yesterday morning."

"That's pretty unusual," Jim replied. "I'd have expected an increase in their communications as they finalize their plans."

"Me, too," Gene admitted. "Bracer has been monitoring every known phone and says they've been completely silent. She believes they've switched to burner phones for this operation."

"What about her voice recognition program?" Jim asked. "Can't she find the new phones that way?"

"Apparently, they're using text messages or some voice alteration system," Gene answered. "We'll keep on top of it and let you know if we find out about anything other than the folks who are waiting for you to leave the parlor. And our plan to counter their efforts remains the same."

"Do we have eyes on our guest?" Jim asked, looking out the window onto the street.

"No. But we have people watching the bridge over the Potomac River that will let us know when they cross," Gene answered. "That'll give them about ten minutes before they arrive. How's it look inside the parlor?"

"Just the Sister and I, along with a single employee that I can see," Jim answered. "I'm sort of wondering if the owner was given some heads up."

"Not that we've heard about," Gene replied. "But without hearing anything for the last twelve hours or so, anything's possible."

"Guess this is pretty much the same as all the other operations you've sent me on," Jim said, taking a glance around the parlor. "Only ten percent of the information I need, and half of what I'm given is wrong."

"That's why you make the big bucks," Gene remarked, laughing. "The cars just entered Virginia. Your next update will probably be when they pull in front of the parlor."

Chapter Twenty-Nine

A few minutes later, Jim heard one of the men watching the van say that the President's cars had just passed the street where he was parked.

"Looks like the game is on," Jim said quietly to Jewell. "Let's hope that everything remains civil."

Seconds later, they saw the two black Suburbans pull to a stop in front of the ice cream parlor. A man wearing a black suit stepped from the lead car and checked up and down the street before stepping into the parlor.

He looked directly at Jim and Jewell for a couple of seconds and then slowly checked the rest of the room. Spotting only the man behind the counter, he spoke into a microphone on his wrist and stepped to the side of the open door.

Through the window beside their table, Jim and Jewell watched as another black-suited man exited the front passenger door and opened the rear door. As he alternated looking up and down the street, the President stepped from the car and walked to the open door of the parlor.

Entering, he walked directly to where Jim and Jewell were sitting. As he neared, Jim and Jewell started to stand,

and he curtly told them, "Keep your seats. I'm not here to indulge in niceties or protocol."

Taking the chair opposite them, he looked at the envelope laying on the table and asked, "Is this the crap you think you can hold over my head? Do you know who you're screwing with? I'm the goddamn President of the United States of America.

And your pathetic attempt at subterfuge, what a joke," he remarked, staring at them. "Do you not think we could figure out that Father Guido Sarducci and Sister Margarita weren't your real names? Let's get this charade over with."

"Mr. President," Jim said quietly. "With all due respect, we know exactly who you are. And yes, that envelope contains photos that are rather disturbing. Pictures of you with young children. And regarding you knowing that Guido and Margarita aren't our real names, that doesn't matter," Jim continued. "The fact is, you don't know our real names. And that's all that matters to us.

We are just the messengers," Jim told him. "What you will see when you open the envelope is what our employers hope will convince you that they are very serious in their requests."

"Have you seen these photos?" the President asked as he slowly slid them out one at a time.

"Yes, sir," I have," Jim answered. "As has Sister Margarita."

The President looked up and asked, "Is this the only set?"

"Of course not," Jim answered, looking directly into his eyes. "I'm sure you wouldn't believe me anyway if I said it was. The organization has the originals of everything."

"These pictures appear to be photoshopped," the President said, shoving the pictures back into the envelope. "I'm going to have my office prove beyond any reasonable doubt that this is just a ploy to interfere with a duly elected official of the United States Government. And I want everything having to do with this operation to disappear or you may just disappear."

"Please, sir, please stay in your seat as I try to convince you that this is a serious situation," Jim told him, holding up both hands. "If you look in the envelope, you'll find an SD card that has the entire three days you spent on the boat on video.

I doubt you could possibly prove the entire video is anything but proof of your actions," Jim continued. "Additionally, the other two days of the five-day cruise have the video of your son Harry with his *cabin attendants*.

We also have the record of the payment from one of the many LLCs you and your son own," Jim told him. "It's not just the photos or the videos, and even if you try to convince the public that the evidence was manufactured, I doubt if you'll survive the fallout."

"Let me tell you a little about fallout," the President said menacingly. "I've buried people like you and your so-called organization a thousand times when they've stood in my way. You will either have *your organization* provide me with proof of the destruction of any *evidence*, or I'll bring the full force of *my organization* down on your heads, and you'll never know it's coming. Do I make myself clear?"

"Respectfully, sir," Jim said, looking up as the President stood. "I don't believe they will do that. I'm asking one final time, please look at this as a most serious issue. But I will report your position as I understand it."

The President leaned over and whispered, "You understand it, you little piece of shit. And you can tell whoever you want whatever you want. But I'll have your ass, as well as everyone else involved in this scheme. Tell that to your people. And I don't make idle threats. You have one week to provide me with what I've asked for, or there won't be another chance. And you won't live another day. Understand that!"

Jim and Jewell sat quietly as the President stormed out of the parlor and headed to his car. As they sat, the agent that had first entered the room stepped up to them and said, "You will remain seated here for five minutes after the car has left. I will be here to ensure you do. Please don't make me take any action that neither of us wants."

"No problem," Jim replied. "We don't want any problems either."

Chapter Thirty

Five minutes later, the Secret Service agent merely nodded at Jim and turned to leave. Once he had entered the car and drove off, Jim heard his team saying, "The van's moving."

As the van slid to a stop in front of the open parlor door, the GMC pickup slammed into the rear and started pushing it down the street. Jim had just started to stand when a man wearing a Dallas Cowboys jersey stepped around from his back, saying, "You're to come with us."

Jim looked at him, looked over his left shoulder at another man with a Texas Rangers jersey, and then asked as he sat back down, "Why should we?"

"Because I've asked nicely," the man said, raising his jersey to show a pistol. "Now, I won't ask nicely again. Stand up slowly and turn around."

Jim looked at Jewell and said, "No, I don't think so. Not even if you ask nicely again," as he slid his right hand down his leg and grasped the pistol pointing almost directly at the man's leg.

As the man in front of him started to reach for his pistol, Jim pulled the pistol loose, pointed it slightly to the right, and pulled the trigger. Quickly standing, he pivoted to his left, where he had seen the other guy, and brought the pistol up and pointed it at his chest.

As the first man fell backward with most of his right leg mangled, the guy behind Jim pulled his pistol out of the front of his pants and tried to swing it toward him.

Jim fired just as the man's pistol was almost pointing at him, catching him directly in the center of his chest. As the guy fell backward, he fired once before hitting the floor.

Jim took a quick look and stepped around the table to where the first man had fallen. Seeing that he was still alive, he kicked his gun away and said, "Houston, we have a problem. I've shot two unknowns, and one is still alive."

Turning back to look at Jewell, he saw her fall to the floor across the body of the man he had shot in the chest. Taking another quick look at the man holding his leg and screaming, Jim stepped back and looked down at Jewell.

Seeing that she had been shot, he then said, "And we have a man down. Get us out of here."

"It was a decoy," someone said as the van accelerated away from the pickup that was pushing it. "A damn decoy!"

"Get back to Jim and Jewell," Gene shouted urgently. "Don't worry about the damn van. Get Jim and her out of there. Bring them here if possible, or get them to the nearest hospital."

"Jewell's going to need a doctor right now," Jim said, looking at her hip where the bullet had struck her. "She's bleeding pretty heavily."

"I'm calling an ambulance," Gene said. "Get the body and other guy out of there. Jim, you stay with Jewell, and we'll figure out how to get you guys back here as soon as Jewell's been taken care of.

I want those other two brought here," Gene continued. "And, make sure the live one remains that way. I want him to answer some questions."

Almost before Gene had finished, the pickup had stopped in front of the parlor, and two of the Black Water agents jumped out, rushing into the room. Seeing the first guy lying on the floor with a puddle of blood beneath his right leg, they pulled him up by his shoulders and dragged him to the pickup.

As they tossed him in the rear seat, another agent used a zip tie to try to stop the blood loss. Rushing back in, they picked up the guy Jim had shot in the chest and took him to the pickup. They tossed him into the rear floorboard. One agent got into the front passenger seat while the agent who had tried to stop the bleeding of the wounded leg stayed in the rear.

The remaining agent stepped back inside and asked, "Do you want me to stay with you in case there's another attempt?"

"No, I don't think so," Jim said as he tried to keep pressure on Jewell's hip. "It would only complicate matters. There's nothing more you can do here. Just go back with the others."

"Ambulance is on its way," Gene told them. "Jim's right. Let's get everyone except him and Jewell out of there. I'll take care of our *guests* when you get them to Quantico."

Jim was breathing hard, but Gene's voice demanded his attention. "Jim, I'll have someone meet you as soon as the ambulance gets you guys to the hospital," Gene said. "I've got a team on their way to talk to the ice cream guy, and we'll figure out what's next as soon as we get everyone's story. Until you hear from me, don't say anything to anyone.

We don't know who to trust right now," Gene continued. "But I promise you this. Whoever those two shooters belong to will be getting a visit. I don't think our employer will be very pleased with this first operation, but that's my problem."

Chapter Thirty-One

When the ambulance arrived at the hospital, Jim sat in the waiting room as the EMT personnel wheeled Jewell down the hall. Less than ten minutes later, Gene came rushing in with two men right behind him.

"How's Jewell?" he asked as Jim stood.

"Don't know," Jim admitted, shaking his head. "They took her directly to one of the operating rooms, and I haven't seen anyone since."

"Did any of the EMTs say anything on the way here?" Gene asked, motioning for Jim to take a seat.

"Not really," Jim answered. "The guy working on her did say that he had stopped the bleeding, but that was about it."

"That's good," Gene replied, nodding. "With luck, the bullet went through without any major damage. At least it appears that it missed the main artery."

"What's going on with the two guys I shot?" Jim asked.

"They were taken to a facility where the guy you shot in the leg is being attended by one of our doctors," Gene told him. "We're trying to identify them right now. I've told one of our best interrogators to stand by to find out what he can from him once the doctor releases him."

"Who do you think they work for?" Jim asked as he watched the doors that led to the operating rooms.

"Harry," Gene told him. "There's no doubt. From the phone calls, after he talked to his dad, there's no chance it's anyone else.

The President may not have had a hand in it, but he pointed Harry in this direction," Gene concluded. "I've notified IL of the meeting and promised him a copy of the conversations we recorded on your phones., along with the recording of the President talking to Harry. I think he'll come to the same conclusion."

"What's our next move?" Jim asked as a doctor in scrubs came through the swinging doors.

Gene watched him approach and said, "I'll tell you when we find out how Jewell's doing."

"Are you gentlemen waiting for news on the Sister that was brought in?" the doctor asked.

"Yes," Jim said, standing. "I'm Father Sarducci, and these are friends of mine. How's Sister Margarita doing?"

"She'll make it," the doctor answered. "The bullet hit her hip bone and did some major damage, but we've got her stabilized, and we're waiting for an orthopedic surgeon to come take a look."

"When can we see her?" Gene asked standing.

"We're moving her to a room in a few minutes once we get everything set up," the doctor answered. "But she'll probably be out of it for at least another hour until the anesthesia wears off. I will have one of the orderlies come get you when we get her in her room."

"Thanks," Jim told him as he turned to leave. "That's good news. Thanks."

Waiting for the doctor to walk through the doors, Gene said, "I'm going to have a meeting with IL this evening.

Unless he has a very convincing argument, I'll tell him that we're moving the deadline up. If the President doesn't agree to resign within three weeks, I'll release the photos."

"What about Harry?" Jim asked. "If you're sure about his involvement, what does the company plan to do? I mean, not only did he try to take us hostage, they tried to kill us."

"We'll know what he directed his guys to do after we talk to the only man we have who knows what Harry told them," Gene replied. "It's possible that they were only told to kidnap you and not harm you."

"Then he should have told them not to come armed," Jim argued. "He should have known that we'd resist. Hell, he could have just told them to follow us and find out where we were.

No, bringing guns meant that they had no intentions of letting us go. Maybe we can't tie this to his dad, but Harry is definitely going to pay for it."

"Let's take care of that when we figure out what IL and the company want," Gene told him. He stood up and put his hand on Jim's shoulder. "For now, let's check in on Jewell and get you back to Texas. There's not much more you can do here."

Chapter Thirty-Two

After flying home most of the night, Jim woke the next morning wondering how Jewell was doing and if there had been any movement toward implementing Gene's plan to move up the deadline regarding the President.

After grabbing a cup of coffee, he carried it into the living room and sat in his recliner before calling Gene's office. When he finally answered, Jim asked, "Two quick questions. How's Jewell, and has the company made any decisions regarding Harry and his father?"

"Good morning," Gene replied. "Nice of you to call and check on the company. First, Jewell will be moved to the same facility that took care of you after you were shot in Fort Worth. She'll be in rehab for a considerable time, but I'm sure she'll recover as well as you did. As to Harry and his father, Harry was certainly behind the attempted kidnapping, and his father was also complicit, as we know from the tapes. Our current guest only knew that they were to take you hostage at any cost. He had no knowledge of Harry's father's involvement or why he was supposed to kidnap you. However, given that you were threatened that you wouldn't live another day if the evidence wasn't destroyed, I believe that he gave tacit approval of whatever Harry did."

"What did IL think about resigning in three weeks?" Jim asked.

"I'm meeting with him again this afternoon," Gene answered. "He wants to look at the impact to the overall picture and how to proceed if he does resign."

"I have a thought," Jim said, sitting his cup on the small table beside his chair. "The President seems to think that he can weather the storm and use all of the power he has to contain us."

Jim paused for a second and then asked, "What if we expose one of the non-political folks first? Let's say that we release the stuff we have on that Baptist Preacher. Don't say anything to the Preacher. Don't give him any chance to wiggle out of it. Just hand everything over to every news organization in the country, especially in Dallas. Don't think IL cares one way or the other about what would happen within one Baptist church here in Texas if it gives him the result he wants with the political folks.

I think that would let the President know that we aren't playing around and are ready to release everything regarding his misadventures in the same manner," Jim finished. "And it would certainly make those we haven't contacted wonder if their heads are about to roll due to their involvement with The Love Boat."

"That's a good idea," Gene agreed. "I'll pass it along when I meet him this afternoon. I don't suppose you'd like to fly back up here and present your idea yourself?"

"I think I've spent enough time on this for now," Jim answered. "I've only got one more day off before I have a trip, and I'm pretty sure Marie sort of expects me to spend a little time with her."

"Tell you what," Gene said. "What if I can convince IL to come with me this afternoon to talk to you? Maybe take him to have dinner with us at Sicilano's?"

"I don't have a problem with that, but do you think it's smart for him to be seen with us?" Jim asked. "After all the secrecy during our first meeting, I'd be very surprised if he agreed to it."

"I think I can assure him that it will go unnoticed," Gene answered. "If you'd just let Marie know that I'm coming to town this evening with an old friend and would love to have him join us for dinner."

"I'll give her a call," Jim said, shaking his head. "But I'll leave the introductions to you if he comes. If he does, or even if he doesn't, you should let Marie know that you'll be leaving immediately after the meal."

"Now, why should I do that?" Gene asked, chuckling. "Does she think I might interrupt some plans she may have for you that don't include me?"

"Let's not test the waters on that," Jim replied. "You can use any story you want, but it should involve leaving tonight … early tonight."

Chapter Thirty-Three

A couple of hours later, Jim had just returned from having breakfast at Denny's when his phone rang. Answering, he heard Gene say that he and the Senator were leaving within the hour and would be landing at Love Field around four o'clock that afternoon.

After the short conversation, he checked his watch to see how much time he had and called Marie. "Good morning," he said as she answered. "How's the day going?"

"Good," she answered. "The girls are coming home this evening for a couple of hours. They were wondering if you'd like to join us for dinner?"

"Sounds perfect," Jim answered. "But there may be a couple of extra folks."

"Let me guess," Marie said. "Gene is coming into town."

"Good guess," Jim replied. "And he's bringing an old friend with him. Do you think the girls would mind if they joined us?"

"I suppose you're not worried about whether or not I'd mind?" Marie asked. "Just what the girls think."

"Of course, I want to know if it would be all right with you," Jim told her. "And with your folks. But I wanted to make sure the girls knew about it also."

Marie was silent for a short period and then said, "Of course, it's all right with me. And I'm sure it will be okay with Mom and Dad. The girls probably don't care either, but I'll let them know. Who is Gene's friend?"

"I've only met him once," Jim answered. "I'll leave it up to Gene to make the introductions since I'm not sure of the connections between them."

"What time do you think they'll be here?" Marie asked.

"They'll land at Love Field about four," Jim answered. "I'm guessing they'll head for a hotel and be here an hour or so later. Say five."

"How about if I tell Dad that we'll be at the restaurant at seven?" Marie asked. "Do you think that will give you enough time?"

"Should be plenty," Jim answered. "I'll see you there at seven."

"The girls will be returning to school after dinner," Marie told him. "Would you like to have some company tonight before you fly out tomorrow?"

"That's probably the best idea I've heard in a long time," Jim answered. "I don't have to be at the airport until eleven, so we won't have to get up too early."

"Good," Marie told him. "I'm assuming you'll be coming to the restaurant with Gene and his friend, so I'll plan on taking you home."

"Anything special you want to do after we get back?" Jim asked.

"Too late for a movie," Marie answered. "How about just a drink on the patio and make it an early night?"

"I'll make a pitcher of Margaritas and have them in the refrigerator," Jim suggested.

"How about some Cuarenta y Tres?" Marie suggested. "I think you said you brought a bottle back from your last trip to Mexico City."

"That I did," Jim replied. "I forgot I had it. Nice after-dinner drink. I'll see you at seven."

Jim spent the rest of the morning and early afternoon doing laundry, cleaning the house, and getting his suitcase ready for the trip the following day. He had just stepped out of the shower when he heard the doorbell ring.

Wrapping a towel around his waist, he headed through the house to the front door. Seeing that it was Gene, he opened the door and said, "You've caught me at a most inopportune time, gentlemen. But, please, come in."

As Gene and the Senator stepped in, Gene said, "I'm sure you remember Senator Knowles."

"Of course, good to see you again, Senator," Jim told him. "I apologize for my appearance, but I ..."

"No problem, son," Jackson interrupted, smiling. "Just hang on to what you've got on so you don't embarrass us all."

"Gene, if you'd take care of the Senator, I'll be right back as soon as I finish dressing," Jim said, leading them into the living room. "You know where everything is."

"I'll take care of it," Gene said, heading for the kitchen. "How about a beer, Jackson?"

Chapter Thirty-Four

Jim grabbed a Ziegen Bock and walked out to join Gene and Jackson on the back porch. As he stepped outside, he asked, "Does anyone need another beer?"

"I think we're good," the Senator said, rising from his chair. "Good to see you again, Jim. And especially fully dressed."

"Good to see you too, sir," Jim replied, shaking his hand. "I didn't expect for you to come all the way down here just to see me, though."

"I like to do things face to face, when possible," Jackson said, sitting back down. "And I especially want to do so when I'm going to disagree with a person."

"I appreciate that," Jim responded, taking a seat. "I just thought it might present a different approach to resolving the problem."

"Your different approach is a good idea," the Senator told him. "I've discussed it with Gene extensively, and we both agree that it's the correct approach after your disastrous first meeting.

And by disastrous, I'm not implying it was in any way your fault," he continued. "It's just that 1 didn't expect the

President's response would be so aggressive. I anticipated resistance, but nothing as violent as what occurred.

And before you ask, I do believe he gave tacit approval," he added. "It's not quite as clear if his son went a little too far, but he ultimately bears the responsibility."

"What is your position on dealing with Harry?" Jim asked, sitting back in his chair.

"We'll get into that at a later date," Jackson answered. "For now, I want to stick to the issue of exposing one of our targets. I said that I disagreed with your proposition. That's probably half an answer. I don't want to use the Baptist Preacher. However, I have another person in mind. Franklin Moss is the Chief Financial Officer, CFO, of a large publicly traded company. And here's my reasoning.

One of my primary goals of this little exposé is to return some of the trust of this country in its institutions," Jackson explained. "Exposing the Preacher's peccadillos would be counter to that.

This country has lost trust in so many of its institutions, including the religious institutions, that it's descending into a moral abyss," he continued. "I don't want to expose a single man's lack of moral values to the detriment of the institution as a whole. I don't care if it's Catholic Priests with Choir Boys or some far-out group that believes in the high priest having the right to sleep with any female before she can marry.

I hope you can understand my point," Jackson concluded. "It's not the approach; it's the target that I want to change."

"I understand," Jim agreed. "I guess I took a narrower view of the operation. I grew up as a Baptist, and I've seen how it's changed over the years. So much so that I haven't returned to any church, and you're correct; further exposure to corruption and hypocrisy would only do more damage."

"Good," Jackson said, standing. "Now, if it's all right with you, I'd enjoy another beer. This Ziegen Bock is pretty damn good. Gene, can I bring you another?"

"Please," Gene answered, setting his empty on the table.

"Moving right along," Gene said as the Senator headed into the house, "I'd like to tell you a little about what the company has done regarding your continued use of the Father Guido Sarducci disguise.

We've retrofitted some of the old files with a character who bears a striking resemblance to him as well as a lady who is an almost perfect match for Sister Margarita," he continued. "Both are members of the CV, or Comando Vermelho, the second largest criminal organization in Brazil. The largest being Primeiro Comando da Captial, or PCC.

If I'm correct in my assumption that the President will continue to attempt to identify both you and Jewell, he'll find you buried within the low levels of CV operatives," he added. "Our intention is to force him to use additional resources and focus his attention outside of the country."

"Not to change the subject," Jim said as Jackson handed Gene a beer and sat down. "But what do you think about demanding the President resign in three weeks or some other short period instead of just announcing his intention not to run for another term?"

Jackson sat back and thought for a moment, then answered, "I'm not so sure that's the correct thing to do. Basically, I really don't want the Vice President to take over. As far as I'm concerned, she's about as ill-equipped to handle the job as a circus monkey.

I think we'd be trading a lame mule for a three-legged donkey," he continued. "I've given it a lot of thought, and I think sticking with the original plan is the appropriate way to proceed. Now, that could change dramatically after we release the story about Franklin Moss's misadventures.

I also think another face-to-face is in order after the fallout from the first exposure hits the fan," Jackson told them. "If his attitude doesn't change, we may revisit the resignation issue."

"What sort of fallout do you think will happen when the first articles hit the streets?" Jim asked.

"Probably initially a stock market disaster for the company," Jackson answered. "The inevitable shakeup at the upper management level. But ultimately, the market will settle down; some people will have made money, and others will lose.

I know you can figure out what stock we're talking about, but it goes without saying," he cautioned, "if you have their stock, hold it. If you don't, don't buy it. That would be considered insider trading and is exactly part of why we're trying to make changes in our institutions. Getting rid of the corruption whether it's moral or financial."

Jim set his empty bottle on the table and stood, saying, "Unfortunately, I guess we'll have to delay resolving the world's dilemmas until after dinner. If we're not at the restaurant on time, I'll have a personal dilemma to handle. And it would quite possibly be worse than this one."

Chapter Thirty-Five

As they walked into the restaurant, Aurora met them saying, "Jim, so good to see you. And Gene, welcome back."

Turning slightly, she continued, "And I'm going to guess this is another new guest. Welcome, sir. Welcome to Siciliano's!"

"Let me introduce my friend, Jackson," Gene said. "Jackson, this is Aurora, the beautiful wife of Anthony, who is by far the most talented chef this side of Sicily."

"Did I just hear a compliment?" Anthony asked as he came from the kitchen. "Of course, it had to be my friend Gene. That other fellow, what's his name … oh, yes. Jim. Thinks my creations are just fine!"

"Tony, my friend Jackson," Gene said, introducing him. "He does hold a grudge. Especially if it's directed at his culinary skills, as Jim can attest."

"Nice to meet you, Anthony," Jackson said, shaking his hand. "I've heard some very complimentary things about this restaurant."

"I'm sure it didn't come from Jim," Tony said, shaking his hand. "Welcome to Siciliano's. And please, make it, Tony. Any friend of Gene is always welcome."

"Where's Marie?" Jim asked quickly, laughing. "I want at least one person here to be glad to see me."

"You know we're all glad to see you, Jim," Aurora told him. "But since you're considered part of the family, you're open to ribbing by my dear husband, Tony."

"I'm not so sure about that," Tony said, putting his arm around Jim's shoulders. "Part of the family, maybe. Glad to see him, maybe not. I've always questioned Marie's choices in men."

"That's enough," Marie said, coming from the dining room. "Let's not subject our new guest to our family's deepest secrets.

Jackson, I'm Marie," she said, extending her hand. "Pay no attention to my family. Now, if you'd please follow me, I'll escort you to Jim's favorite table."

As they took their seats, Marie told them, "I've set out a bottle of Dad's favorite red wine. I hope you'll enjoy it. I'll be right back with some fresh bread and butter while Dad makes your salads."

"Did I miss something, or did we already order?" Jackson asked as Marie left the table.

"Tony orders for us," Gene answered as he poured a glass of wine for Jackson. "I'm not sure if we're guinea pigs for a new dish or he's made too much of something and needs to get rid of it."

"Doesn't matter," Jim replied, taking a glass from Gene. "I've never had anything that wasn't delicious."

"Delicious or just fine?" Marie asked, smiling as she set the plate of bread, butter, and marinara sauce on the table.

"See what I have to put up with," Jim said as Marie kissed his cheek. "I feel like Rodney Dangerfield, 'No respect. I get no respect. By the way, do you know what Tony is making us for dinner this evening?"

"Lasagna," she answered as she turned to go. "His most famous *just fine* creation."

As she was leaving, Aurora brought in three plates piled high with Caesar salads. Setting them on the table, she told them that Marie would be in shortly with the main course.

Moments later, Marie brought in a large platter covered with steaming lasagna. Setting it in the center of the table, she said, "Please serve yourselves, gentlemen. Dad said he will join you for a drink after you finish your meal if that's okay with you. Will there be anything else?"

"Maybe you need to bring in a family of twelve to help us eat this," Jackson joked as Gene slid a chunk of the lasagna onto his plate. "I'm sure that there are communities in Italy that could live for weeks on this much food."

"Dad believes no one should ever leave hungry," Marie told him, putting her hand on Jim's shoulder. "As he always says, 'Man can live without shoes, but not nourishment.' Please, enjoy."

As they were taking their second helping, Jackson took his phone from his pocket, checked who was calling, and said, "Excuse me, but I've got to take care of this."

Sliding his chair back, he answered, "Go ahead."

Holding the phone to his ear, he headed toward the exit, listening but not saying a word.

"Something wrong?" Marie asked, walking back in.

"No," Jim told her. "Just an unexpected call. I'm sure he'll be right back."

"I hope it doesn't interrupt your evening," she replied, looking from Jim to Gene. "Dad's making a special dessert for you guys, so please save a little room for that."

Chapter Thirty-Six

Marie had returned to the kitchen when Jackson walked back in. Looking around the room to ensure there weren't any new patrons, he took his seat and said, "The information on Franklin Moss will be released early in the morning."

Jim and Gene exchanged looks, and Jim asked, "How explosive is this going to be?"

"Hiroshima would be an apt comparison," Jackson said, taking a bite of his lasagna. "Probably a combination of Hiroshima and Nagasaki at the same time."

"How soon will it hit the presses?" Gene asked.

"I have people with direct access to every news organization," Jackson replied. "They will make sure that it's a headline on every print and the lead story on every television network. So, when the papers hit the streets in the morning, it will be there."

"How much of Franklin's actions are going to be seen?" Jim asked as he wondered how explicit it would be.

"Everything except sexually explicit photos or videos or faces of the children," the Senator answered. "But there will be no doubt about Franklin's activities."

"How's this going to impact the operation down in Brazil and in Hawaii?" Gene asked, knowing that everything was in place to remove the leaders of the Comando Vermelho who were involved with the Barco Do Amor operation.

"It'll have to be ready to go tomorrow," Jackson answered. "I'm not positive that a single exposure will be enough to cause a ripple in their operation, but if your people see anything that would preclude a future resolution to the situation, you have the authority to execute whatever plans you have in place."

"What are the plans for the Brazilian operation?" Jim asked.

"We'll eliminate the members of CV that are involved with the Love Boat," Gene answered.

"Why not the leaders of CV?" Jim asked. "Won't they just start another operation?"

"Probably," Gene answered. "But we're not going to get involved with Brazil's problem. And, sometimes, it's nice to have two separate criminal organizations competing with each other.

Our goal in this operation is to expose the activities of our people, not determine the moral values of other countries," he continued. "Besides, the cost of an operation that tried to eradicate CV would be astronomical. And outside the scope of our contract with the Senator."

"And Honolulu?" Jim asked. "What's my involvement, and how soon do I need to be ready?"

"Same answer," Gene replied. "Let's see what happens after the news hits. We have a team that'll schedule a cruise when we're ready to eliminate the yacht and its crew."

"I can't imagine Black Water sanctioning a sex cruise," Jim argued. "And I can't imagine one of our people wanting to be involved."

"The cruise is for three couples," Gene explained. "The cover is that they are involved in group activities, and that is why they won't have any cabin attendants involved.

All six people are members of Muddy Water, not married to each other, and will be taken from the yacht before it's sent to Davy Jones's locker," he finished.

"Then what's my involvement?" Jim asked.

"You're one of the men out for a five-day cruise with your wife and two other like-minded couples. Matter of fact, you're the man who organized the cruise," Gene answered. "And no, Jewell was never considered to be part of this operation even if she hadn't been shot."

"I have to ask again: why are we exterminating this particular part of their operation if we aren't going after the head of the snake?" Jim asked, shaking his head.

"Let me answer that," Jackson said, looking at Gene.

Turning to Jim, he continued, "I don't give a rat's ass what those people do in any other part of the world. Hell, they can run sex cruises for monkeys out of Playa de Puta for all I care.

But when they bring their crap to the shores of America, our laws and values take precedence over whatever lifestyle they want to pursue elsewhere," he said. "Now, every asset they have that's involved in operations out of any US territory is going to be destroyed. Maybe it won't stop their activities, but they'll damn sure think twice before they use my country to do it again.

Does that answer your question?" the Senator asked pointedly. "That boat and crew violated our sovereign nation and will face the consequences."

"Understood," Jim said, nodding. "I've got no problem with that. But I at least hope my partner is cute as hell if I have to spend five days on a boat with her."

Chapter Thirty-Seven

Jim had just gotten home from his three-day trip when his phone rang.

Answering, he heard the familiar voice of Gene saying, "Welcome home. Do you have any plans for the next three days?"

"Well, I'd like to have a day or two to spend with Marie, maybe go to a movie, have a quiet dinner at home, do laundry, clean house, wash the 'Vette, mow the yard, but that's about all," Jim answered. "But I'm guessing you have other plans for my preciously few days off."

"Only for a day or two," Gene replied. "How about if I have a plane at Love Field tomorrow evening about, let's say, seven o'clock to bring you to Quantico."

"I'm guessing again that this has something to do with a certain Franklin Moss," Jim said.

"Not really," Gene answered. "Except that the release of his activities has been an impetus to a larger issue. One that you're intimately familiar with."

"Another guess … someone who wants another meeting with Father Sarducci," Jim said.

"You're getting good at this guessing game," Gene said, laughing. "But let's return to the problem at hand. Our respected party insists on a meeting in two days and has tendered an offer that we need to explore."

"What sort of offer is he making?" Jim asked as he pulled on a pair of Wrangler jeans.

"You know I can't discuss that on the phone," Gene told him. "But you'll get a detailed briefing on the flight from Love to Quantico."

"Is there going to be another Sister with me this time?" Jim asked, pulling on his boots.

"No," Gene answered. "Our party knows that there is no Children of El Barco, so there's no need to continue that charade."

"Who am I going as this time?" Jim asked, pulling on a T-shirt.

"Still, Father Sarducci," Gene told him. "There's no need to try to disguise you as anyone else and provide them with more photos of another you that could lead them to discover your identity.

And that's another reason to keep this meeting to just you," Gene finished. "We don't need to risk exposure of another agent."

"Understand," Jim replied, heading for the kitchen. "What about another attempt on me?"

"That was brought up," Gene told him. "And it was explained in graphic detail what would happen if anything like that happened again."

"Did he deny his involvement?" Jim asked, taking a Ziegen Bock from the refrigerator.

"Of course," Gene answered. "But we assured him that any further attempt on you, whether on his part or that of any other party, will result in the immediate release of the material.

He has assured us that he guarantees your complete safety," Gene finished.

"As if I feel entirely secure," Jim responded, heading outside to the back porch. "But, there's not much more we can do. Where's the meeting this time?"

"Same ice cream parlor," Gene answered. "But I'm sure there will be a more thorough check of the facility before he arrives. So yes, there's not much more we can do to ensure your safety."

"At least we're not risking anyone else's life," Jim said, sitting down at the table. "How's Jewell doing?"

"As well as can be expected," Gene answered. "The orthopedic surgeon said there should be no permanent disabilities, but her hip will probably take some time to heal and require extensive physical therapy."

"That I know only too well, as does she," Jim replied. "But then there's that old saying about broken eggs and making an omelet."

"Unfortunately," Gene said. "But I don't like putting anyone at greater risk than absolutely necessary."

"Agreed," Jim said, taking a sip of his beer. "But there's always a risk. Even just driving to Denny's for breakfast."

"I wondered how you'd work omelets and risk into a conversation," Gene told him, laughing. "Now, if you don't mind, I've got a million things that I need to take care of before your meeting in two days. I'll see you at Love Field tomorrow evening. Enjoy your evening with Marie."

Chapter Thirty-Eight

"Hey, Marie," Jim said as she answered his call. "Do you have any plans for this evening?"

"You better believe it," she answered immediately. "I plan on ravaging you until you can't take any more. How's that for a plan?"

"That sounds like a damn good plan," Jim responded, laughing. "But you do know that the success of any good plan is attention to detail. So, just what are the details?"

"Oh, no," Marie told him, laughing. "I can't divulge the details. You're just going to have to wait. But you can speculate all you want."

"I'll give it some thought," Jim replied. "How about if I cook dinner and grab a movie?"

"I believe I can work that into my plan," she answered. "As long as it's not *The Cure for Insomnia*."

"I can guarantee you it won't be since I've never heard of it," Jim told her.

"It was released a few years ago," she explained, laughing. "The film ran for 85 hours! From January 31 to February 3, 1987!"

"I was thinking about Little Shop of Horrors," Jim said. "It's only about an hour and a half."

"I guess that'll work," Marie replied. "But don't blame me if we have to use the pause button repeatedly."

"Now that that's settled, I'll have everything ready to cook when you get here," Jim told her. "Then it'll only take about ten minutes."

"What are you planning?" she asked.

"Scallops and shrimp tempura," Jim answered. "I've got a special sauce that I make, a bottle of sake, and chopsticks. Plus, clean-up is quick and easy."

"Sounds delicious," Marie replied. "Can I bring anything?"

"Just a smile," Jim answered. "How's five o'clock sound?"

"No problem," she answered. "Are you sure you can wait that long to see me?"

"It'll be tough, but I'll handle it," Jim told her, laughing.

"Just don't handle it too much," she teased. "Leave that for me."

"I think we better change the subject," Jim told her, laughing. "Is there anything else you want? Dessert? Wine?"

"Nope," she said. "Now, should we discuss tomorrow and your plans?"

"I guess now is as good a time as ever," Jim answered. "I have to be at Love Field tomorrow evening at about seven o'clock. But I don't have any plans other than that."

"What's going on at Love Field?" she asked. "Does this have something to do with Gene and that other guy who came to dinner at the restaurant the other day?"

"Yes," Jim answered. "There seems to be some sort of issue with some changes that the client wants to make, so

Gene asked me to come to sit in on the review to see what impact it would have."

"How long will you be gone?" she asked, her disappointment evident in her voice.

"I should be back the next evening if everything goes as planned," Jim answered. "Hopefully, in time for dinner with you. Do you think Tony could be talked into making his shrimp scampi?"

"I'm sure I can put in a good word," Marie answered. "But it'll cost you."

"Doesn't it always," Jim replied. "But money well spent."

"I'm not talking about money, silly boy," Marie corrected him. "I'm talking about your time. You're gone three or four days a week with the airlines, and then Gene needs you every time you have some days off … I want equal time."

"I'll work on that," Jim said. "If I had my way, you'd get more than equal time; you'd get at least sixty percent."

"You're such an ass, Jim Lashley," Marie told him. "But I'll put up with it … for now. But one of these days, we need to have a serious discussion about your and Gene's *Guy Time*.

By the way," she continued. "That guy who came with Gene, I believe his name was Jackson. Isn't he some sort of politician or something?"

"Yeah," Jim answered. "He's got something to do with the contract that we've been discussing. I hope this meeting resolves it. And that might resolve your concern about having equal time.

However," he continued. "If equal time is what you really want, you're aware that if I spend less time with Gene, to be equal, I'd have to spend less time with you as well."

"Have I mentioned that you're an ass?" Marie asked.

"I believe so. And I'll probably be hearing it again," Jim answered, laughing. "Anyway, I've got to get my ass moving if I'll have everything ready when you get here. I'll see you at five."

Chapter Thirty-Nine

After telling Marie goodbye the next morning and having taken her to a late breakfast, Jim started repacking his suitcase for the next trip for American Airlines, knowing that his one or two-day trip to Quantico could extend into three and he would have little spare time to get home and make it to the airport for the trip.

Tossing it into his pickup so it would be at Love Field when he got back, he returned to the house and packed another bag with three pairs of underwear, socks, and T-shirts for the Quantico trip.

Satisfied that as long as he got back to Love Field by ten o'clock for his flight from DFW to Denver, he shouldn't have any difficulties. That was unless some abnormal traffic situation occurred between Love Field and DFW. Always a possibility.

A couple of hours later, after doing two loads of laundry, Jim took his overnight bag, climbed in his pickup, and headed for Love Field. The mental game of trying to imagine how this new meeting with the President would go kept him occupied until he parked and walked to the General Aviation terminal.

As he walked into the terminal, he noticed a white Gulfstream IV taxiing onto the parking ramp. Nodding to the lady behind the desk, he said, "Looks like my ride is a little early."

"That must mean you're also early," she replied with a smile. "Do you need a ride out to the plane?"

"No, ma'am," Jim answered, watching the ground crew marshaling the plane to a stop. "But, with your permission, I'll go on out and get aboard."

"No problem," she told him, smiling. "When will you be coming back?"

"Two or three days," Jim answered, noticing the flirtatious look. "Hopefully not longer than that."

"I hope you have a good trip," she said, leaning over the counter slightly. "Don't forget to stop in and say hello."

"Definitely," Jim told her as he opened the double glass door leading out onto the ramp. "You have a great day as well."

As he walked toward the plane, the stairs came out from the left side and Gene was standing at the top watching him approach. "Been waiting long?" he asked as Jim started up the stairs.

"Just got here," Jim said, shaking Gene's hand. "How's it going with things up north?"

"It's turning into a shit-storm," Gene answered, leading him to the seats toward the rear. "The news media is flogging Mr. Moss with a cat 'o nine tails hourly. If you ever wanted to start something, this is probably your finest hour."

"I wouldn't say I started this," Jim replied taking a seat facing Gene. "I merely suggested letting our current target see that we're serious."

"Well, no matter what you say, the company and our friend believe this is your handiwork," Gene argued. "Now, they may never say it, but they are extremely pleased with the outcome."

"As long as it moves us to what we were tasked with, I'll accept either the blame or laudable praise," Jim said. "But I still think the Baptist Preacher would have made a great first revelation."

"Don't tell me you're quoting the bible now," Gene replied, smiling. "I'm even surprised that you'd know anything about the book of Revelation."

"That wasn't a reference to anything in particular," Jim explained, shaking his head. "Just an off-the-cuff comment."

"Unintentional it may have been, but using the word revelation in context with a Baptist Preacher's hypocrisy, that's got to be a Freudian slip," Gene said, laughing. "But we've come up with a name for this operation. Would you like to know what it is?"

"Go ahead," Jim answered. "I'm sure the company spent countless hours to come up with a name that obfuscates the intent of the operation. Maybe some acronym like MADD for May All Deviants Die."

"Not even close," Gene said as the stairs retracted into the plane and the door closed.

"I can't wait to hear," Jim said as the Captain came walking back toward their seats.

"Everything is ready," he told Gene. "If there's nothing else, we'll get on our way."

"We're good back here," Gene told him. "Just give us a heads up if there are any problems."

"Absolutely," the Captain told him. "And give me a call if we can do anything to make your flight more enjoyable."

Waiting for the Captain to enter the cockpit, he turned to Jim with a deadpan look on his face and said, "Operation Shit-storm."

"I'm almost surprised that you didn't try to make it Jim's Shit-storm," Jim replied, looking at the floor slowly shaking his head as the engines started.

"That may have been brought up by the Senator," Gene told him, laughing. "Seems he has a sense of humor that rivals even yours."

Chapter Forty

"Okay, what sort of offer has he made?" Jim said once they were taxiing out for takeoff.

"He's willing to promise us he won't run again," Gene answered. "But, he's not willing to publicly announce that he's not going to run after this term."

"What does our Senator think?" Jim asked as the engines spooled up, entering the runway.

"He's not too surprised," Gene answered. "But he sees it as a sort of chink in his armor. Maybe he's worried enough that he's considered taking the original offer but thinks he can negotiate a better deal."

"What do you think?" Jim asked as they accelerated down the runway.

"Probably the same as you do," Gene answered. "I wouldn't trust his word for a second. The man is a politician. He'll tell you anything that he thinks you want to hear."

"I'd bet you're right," Jim said as the plane curved east and climbed away from the airport. "What about any development regarding any of the other patrons of the Love Boat?"

"Nothing concrete," Gene told him. "But there have been a couple of cancellations for future cruises, according to our team down in Brazil. Word must be spreading, and it wouldn't surprise me if some people weren't on our list leaving their jobs due to family emergencies."

"That's fine with me," Jim agreed, nodding. "That means I don't have to deal with as many scumbags. Even though I must confess that it gives me a certain perverse pleasure to watch them squirm when I present them with proof of their child molestation.

But I'll take them leaving so I'm not tempted to slap the shit out of them just for general purposes," he finished.

"I understand," Gene agreed. "Another issue that could present itself is the public outrage and demand for the release of any names associated with the Barco Do Amor should too many public officials be exposed."

"Personally, I'd love to see the list printed in every newspaper or broadcast on every network," Jim replied. "But I know that would show the world how the sausage is made."

"Not to mention that some of the patrons of the cruises have no idea of what others did on their cruise," Gene told him. "It would stigmatize people who just wanted to enjoy some time at sea with someone special. Or maybe a company-sponsored trip for some executives and their wives.

We can't paint everyone with that brush," he continued. "And that's not what the company is tasked with. Let's just keep the cesspool of people we have to deal with at a minimum."

Nodding his agreement, Jim asked, "What has the company done regarding the meeting? I know the President was told that he'd be held responsible if anything happened again. But, like trusting him on his word regarding not running for a second term, I can more imagine him trying to gain some leverage to force the company, or the Children of the Boat, to turn over any material that proves what he did.

The man doesn't care who or how many he hurts," Jim continued. "He's a compulsive liar and has proven to be ruthless. I'm sure I'll be searched, as well as the parlor, before I arrive. But I'm hoping the company has some backup in case shit heads south."

"We've looked at every aspect of an attempt to harm or kidnap you," Gene assured him. "We've placed cameras throughout the parlor and on every conceivable location that has a visual on the surrounding blocks.

We'll have cars located on every block in each direction for five blocks," he continued. "They'll have spike strips, and we'll block every intersection. But that's only possible if the President and his security detail have left the area."

"If it was me," Jim responded, "I'd plan on that and have exactly the same type of vehicle the President uses. Bulletproof glass and puncture-proof tires."

"So would I," Gene agreed. "But we can push this only so far when we're dealing with what could be construed as an attempt on the President. Sorry, but there's definitely some risk here that falls on your shoulders."

Pausing to let it sink in, he continued, "And it's always your decision as to where to draw the line on any mission. The same here."

"No," Jim said immediately. "I'm meeting with the worthless asshole, and I'll worry about what comes next when it happens. I'll deal with it then."

Chapter Forty-One

The next morning, Jim was again dressed as Father Sarducci and had just finished checking his phone was connected to Black Water operations and his earpiece was functioning correctly.

"Ready to go," Gene asked, nodding his approval at the change in Jim's appearance.

"As I'll ever be," Jim answered as he adjusted his Biretta. "Has there been any activity around the parlor this morning?"

"A four-man team, who we assume belong to the President's security detail, arrived almost an hour ago," Gene answered. "They spent about fifteen minutes checking the place out and left. We were monitoring them with the cameras we installed yesterday as they searched the parlor with special attention to the table where you were last time."

"What about strange vehicles, like vans?" Jim asked, adjusting his bulletproof vest beneath his robe.

"Nothing we can identify that's anything other than normal traffic since we stationed cars in the area," Gene told him. "We're as confident as we can be that this won't be a repeat of the last meeting."

"Good," Jim said, nodding. "Then, let's get this over with. I'd really like to get home tonight and have a little time before I have to leave tomorrow."

"By all means, let's go," Gene responded, heading for the door. "The teams that are already there will give us any updates of newly arriving vehicles, and Bracer's folks will keep us apprised of the President's approach."

Twenty minutes later, as they pulled to the front of the ice cream parlor, they heard that the President had just left 1600 Pennsylvania Avenue.

"About fifteen minutes," Gene told Jim as he checked him out before he got out of the Suburban. "Any last-minute questions or ideas?"

"Not that anyone can answer at this point," Jim said. "But I don't think he's going to take a no to his offer very well."

"I'm sure he won't," Gene agreed as he checked up and down the street. "Just keep in mind that you're not there to convince him of any decision. Just to relay that his offer is insufficient. Also, if he modifies his offer, he needs to understand that you can only relay it, not approve it."

Jim reached for the door handle and said, "Got it. Here's where the 'Don't shoot the messenger' saying becomes important.

I'm going in," Jim said, opening the door. "I'm having a double scoop of Pistachio Almond ice cream. And the company is picking up the tab."

"I'll come in and join you after the meeting is over," Gene said, leaning over to look at Jim as he got out. "And I'll use actual cash instead of the company credit card."

"But I bet you'll ask for a receipt and include the charge on your expense report, though," Jim said, bending over and looking at Gene.

"What does it matter to you?" Gene asked, laughing. "You'll be getting free ice cream."

"I just wish they had Blue Bell ice cream," Jim told him, laughing. "But free ice cream is about the best thing I can think of concerning this meeting."

Just then, they heard the notification that their party was less than ten minutes out. "I'll be fine," Jim said, shutting the car door. "I just hope the man doesn't piss me off enough to make me say something stupid."

"You say something stupid?" Gene replied as Jim walked away. "Now, when has that ever happened?"

Chapter Forty-Two

Jim was about halfway through with his small bowl of ice cream when the first black-suited man entered and stood in the doorway, surveilling the room. After a quick look, he stepped to the side and spoke into a microphone on his wrist.

Two more identically dressed men entered and walked to where Jim was sitting. "Would you please stand up?" the first one to the table asked as the other went around behind him.

"Of course," Jim answered, placing his spoon in the bowl and pushing his chair back.

"Now, please raise your arms," the man in front of him directed as Jim rose from his seat.

Once Jim's arms were raised, the man behind him did a quick but thorough pat down and then nodded to the other man.

"You can take your seat," the man in front told him. "But, please keep your hands on the table in front of you until the President departs."

"Of course," Jim replied as the man at the door looked outside and nodded.

Seconds later, the President entered the parlor and walked directly to where Jim was sitting. "Where's the Sister?" he asked sarcastically as he took his seat.

"She had pressing obligations elsewhere," Jim answered, now seeing how this was going to be. "But I'll tell her you asked."

"Enough bullshit," the President said menacingly. "What's the answer to my offer?"

"I'm afraid the answer is no," Jim said flatly. "No disrespect to the office, but your word alone is insufficient."

"My word is insufficient?" the President growled. "I'm not the one hiding behind some elaborate charade with costumes and fake identities.

Yeah, I know that you're tied to that Brazilian criminal organization CV," he continued. "Does it surprise you that we'd identify you sooner rather than later? It shouldn't. You're nothing but a low-level cartel flunkie. And you don't trust my word? What a crock of crap.

If your boss, or whoever is pulling your strings, isn't satisfied with my offer, what does he have to offer?" he asked, sitting back.

"He has no further offers," Jim said, leaning forward and putting his elbows on the table. "I'm just here to tell you that there is only one offer, the initial offer. You either publicly announce that you won't be running for a second term, or the details of your days at sea will be released."

"I can't just do that," the President said, leaning back. "That would place the entire political system in chaos. Can't you people see that?

Hell, I'd be a lame-duck President the second I make the announcement," he continued. "The government would come to a standstill for the remainder of my term. Is that what you people are after? Shutting down the United States government? For what reason?"

"Sir, if I'm not mistaken, you're the one who opted for the little boat ride you took," Jim said, staring at him. "Do you think that because of your position, you'd be immune from the consequences?

And as far as shutting down the government, I'm pretty sure the country can function without a man whose morals are certainly questionable if not downright repulsive," Jim continued. "But, I'm not here to judge you. As far as I'm concerned, that's why your country has elections.

And I'd be willing to bet that the country will survive even if the information is released," Jim said, leaning back and leaving his hands flat on the table. "But, can you survive if it's released? Seems to me your choices both amount to the same thing.

You try to ride it out, and the information will surely result in your removal in disgrace," Jim told him. "And that would certainly be worse than being a lame duck. No, sir, the only logical choice is to make the announcement and finish out your term with some amount of respect remaining.

But, again, I'm just here as the messenger," Jim finally told him. "I was sent here to provide you with the answer to your offer. Nothing more. Nothing less.

Now that you've given me your answer, I'll relay it to my superior," Jim concluded.

"Wait just a minute," the President hurriedly said. "I never said I wouldn't make the announcement."

"Really?" Jim asked, leaning forward. "Correct me if I'm wrong, but didn't you just say, and I quote, 'I can't just do that'? What was that, some sort of dance around an actual answer?

In my world, when a man says he can't do something, that means either he can't … or he won't," Jim continued. "So, what did you mean? I certainly don't want to convey the wrong information or the incorrect response to whether or not you intend to make your announcement."

"It's that I can't just do it immediately," the President replied in an attempt to recover. "I'd like a week to see how much of an impact this would make and try to find a way to minimize it."

Jim sat quietly for a few seconds and then said, "Very well. I'll let them know you want another week to decide how to protect your, let's say, reputation."

The President pushed his chair back and looked at Jim before saying, "You may think you have the situation under control. But you severely underestimate both me and my office. You report whatever you want. But I demand to be given the week I requested. Make sure your people understand that sonny boy."

Chapter Forty-Three

Mere seconds after the last of the President's security guard had left the parlor Gene came in and headed for Jim's table.

"The Senator wants to see us at Quantico," he said as he looked at the now-melted ice cream. "We had him listening to the meeting, and he's just a little pissed."

"Guess we better go then," Jim said as he pushed back his chair. "Any idea what he plans?"

"No, but I wouldn't be surprised if he authorized the release of the information tonight," Gene answered as they left the parlor.

"Why does he need to see me?" Jim asked as they got into the Suburban. "I just presented the facts as I was directed."

"I certainly don't know," Gene told him as he started the car. "Hell, I don't know why he needs to see either of us. He heard the same thing I did, and since you were there, you know as much as either of us."

"I guess since he's paying the bills, so to speak, he can make the rules," Jim replied as they headed east.

After clearing the gates and security, Gene led Jim to one of the soundproof meeting rooms where the Senator was reviewing the list of those members of Congress who had been on the Love Boat.

"Take a seat," he told them as he finished looking at the list. "If that arrogant bastard thinks he can wiggle out of this, he's wrong. He's about to get an education."

Laying down the list, he looked at Jim and asked, "What do you think he intends to do, based on the meeting?"

Jim thought for a moment and then answered, "I'd bet he thinks he can claim this is some phony story concocted to disrupt his Presidency. Maybe something like a plot by Russia to interfere with whatever the President is doing regarding some international agenda.

I'd bet that right now, he's having photos made that show him and his son at one of his homes," Jim added. "And, if it was me, I'd toss in pictures of other family members and include a few of the Secret Service agents in the background.

I'd make sure the date and time stamps coincide with the boat trip and doctor the agent's logs to show they were at the same location," Jim concluded. "Hell, some people still believe the moon landing was actually some video shot behind a hill in Nevada. I'm sure he thinks he can spin this to his advantage."

"What would you do?" Jackson asked Jim.

"First, get copies of all of the files regarding every agent's location, duty periods, or anything else that can prove where they really were," Jim answered. "Then, I'd release the name and information of one member of Congress that was involved.

And I'd do it immediately," Jim continued. "No offer to let him step down. No warning. Just let it hit the news.

I don't know if that will make any difference," Jim said, looking directly at Jackson. "But it'll damn sure be another shot across his bow. Especially since it will come out of nowhere and be as unsuspected to whoever you pick."

"That's pretty much what I thought," Jackson said, picking up the list. "I've narrowed it down to two members of the house. Both are Democrats. Both have been in Congress for over thirty years. The only difference is one is from a state with a Republican governor, and the other is from a state with a Democratic governor."

"It's not my decision," Jim replied. "But since your goal has been to have as little impact on the balance as possible, I think the logical choice is door number two since he's more likely to appoint a Democratic replacement."

"I know you're correct," Jackson told him, shaking his head. "The shame of it is that he's also been one of my friends for many years. Hell, I was at his daughter's wedding just a few years ago. His wife and mine have been friends for even longer. This is going to be a shock to every one of them."

"Except him," Jim said quietly. "He put them in this position. I'm sorry he's your friend, but it's not your problem. At least not if you make the decision, I believe you're going to make."

Jackson looked at Gene and asked, "What do you think, General?"

Gene thought for a second and then answered, "Sir, I'm afraid I have to agree with Jim. It's one of the most difficult decisions a man has to make.

But when a man gets what he deserves, no matter how close he is to you, that's always the right choice," Gene told him. "I've had to make the same decision many times regarding people who worked for me in the past. Good officers. And like this, some close friends. But men who crossed the line of acceptable behavior.

That's one of the problems with being in charge," Gene concluded. "You get to make the tough decisions knowing the outcome won't be pleasant."

Chapter Forty-Four

"Can both of you wait here for a couple of minutes?" Jackson asked, laying the list on the table. "I've got to make a quick phone call."

"No problem," Gene replied. "Is there anything you need us to do?"

"Just wait," Jackson answered, heading for the door.

"What do you think he wants us to wait for?" Jim asked as the Senator closed the door behind him.

"I'd say to let us know that he hung his old friend out to dry," Gene answered.

"I hope he doesn't take too long," Jim said. "I'm still hoping to get home this afternoon so I can take care of a few things before my flight tomorrow."

Less than five minutes later, Jackson came back in and told them, "It's done. News of my friend's misdeeds will be released immediately and in everybody's home by ten o'clock tonight.

And, I ordered the complete logs for the Presidential Security Detail for the last year," he added. "Now, I'm sure the President will hear of the release within the hour and have no doubt that he'll be informed of my requests for the logs.

I have no doubt that he'll be contacting the Brazilian Embassy shortly after he understands that we aren't just sitting around waiting for him to dictate terms," Jackson concluded.

"What do you think he'll try to do?" Gene asked.

"Set up another meeting," Jackson answered. "He's smart enough to understand that the quick release of the congressman's information and the request were meant to force his hand."

"How soon do you anticipate that?" Gene asked, looking from him to Jim.

"Within the day," Jackson told him. "I know this may disrupt some plans, but I need both of you ready to meet with him when he calls."

"Not a problem," Gene replied before looking at Jim. "I'll take care of making sure that we're at your disposal."

"Guess you're going to contact the company and have someone mysteriously need my flight for tomorrow," Jim responded, shaking his head.

"Actually, I'm going to contact one of the pilots that's on reserve who wants to use your flight to maintain his landing currency," Gene answered. "And I'm sure his request will be granted."

"Guess that leaves me with only one other issue to explain," Jim said. "I'm not sure how Marie is going to take this since she's already making noises about the amount of time I spend with you."

"Maybe she'll be even happier if you have three or four days off to spend with her," Gene suggested. "She was only going to get one day, maybe just part of one day, and then you were going to be gone for three."

"Sometimes I don't think it's the number of days, just that if she doesn't get the ones she expects, that becomes the issue," Jim replied.

"What if I bring her out here?" Gene suggested. "I'll get you guys a room, and you can take her sightseeing until the meeting is over. Then, I'll fly back with you."

"This might take a few days," Jim reminded him. "I'm not sure what she has planned."

"Well, she can fly out and spend whatever time she wants, and I'll fly her home," Gene argued. "I don't know what else we can do."

"I'll call her and explain that things aren't going well with the contract, that I could be here for three or four more days, and that I'd like her to come out," Jim replied.

"That should work," Gene agreed. "Now, I've got to make a call and get you off the schedule with American."

"And I need to make that call to Marie," Jim said, standing and heading for the door.

"Tell you guys what," Jackson said, following them to the door. "I'm going to check in and see if the fur is about to fly with our revisions. What say we meet back here in thirty minutes?"

"Sounds good," Gene said, holding the door for the Senator. "Give us a chance to grab a bite. If you hear anything sooner, we'll be in the cafeteria."

Chapter Forty-Five

After they returned to the meeting room thirty minutes later, Jackson announced, "The Congressman from Idaho has resigned. And more importantly, we have another meeting tomorrow morning at eight o'clock with our primary party.

Jim, you are authorized to explain to the President that he has wasted much of his time trying to intimidate you and us and that the week he asked for is unacceptable," he said. "We are prepared to give him three days, starting tomorrow, for him to formally announce his intentions of not seeking a second term."

"So, you're willing to accept his word this time?" Jim asked.

"Yes, as far as what he said he wanted, a week to find a way to minimize the impact of his announcement," Jackson answered. "He wanted a week; we're offering three days.

And, let him be assured that on the eve of the third day, if no announcement has been made, everything will be released, including the videos," he finished.

"Where's the meeting?" Jim asked as he thought about the enormity of what was about to happen.

"Same as before," the Senator answered.

Turning to Gene, he said, "I want that place under surveillance beginning immediately and any additional cameras throughout the area to ensure we see anyone coming anywhere near it.

I don't want another attempt on Jim," he explained. "If that asshole President thinks he can do anything to disrupt this, I wouldn't put it past him to try the most outrageous acts. Even if he knows the futility of taking Jim, he may just do it anyway. Remember, desperate people take desperate measures."

"I'll take care of it as soon as we leave," Gene assured him,

Turning to looking at Jim, he asked, "Can you think of anything else to make sure you're covered?"

"Putting another person or couple in the parlor? Perhaps replacing the guy behind the counter?" Jim suggested.

"I don't think we have time to coordinate the counter guy's replacement," Gene answered. "But I can have a couple of our people show up while you're in the meeting.

The security detail probably won't let them in, but they'll still be there," Gene explained. "And, they'll be armed as well as the cars we deployed through the area last time.

Not to change the subject, but what did Marie say about coming out?" Gene asked.

"She said she can't make it tomorrow, but if we'll still be here the next day, she'd love to come," Jim answered. "Do you think we'll still be here?"

"I want both of you here for the next three days," Jackson said. "It wouldn't surprise me if he doesn't ask for another meeting after tomorrow and another the next day.

You've got to realize that he's fighting for his life," he continued. "Not his physical life … his political life. And I think that's more important to him than his physical life.

I think it's only fair to be available for us to be ready to meet with him whenever he requests," Jackson added after a short pause. "He is the President of the United States, and we must respect the office regardless of who holds it.

Hell, I'm sorry this has to happen," Jackson said, shaking his head. "Almost as sorry as I was with my friend. But no man, not even the most powerful man in the world, can flaunt social morals without some repercussions. No one."

"Well, sir, if there's nothing else to discuss here, I need to get things going for tomorrow," Gene said, looking at Jackson.

"Not that I can think of," the Senator said, rising from his chair. "I'll be back in the morning before Jim leaves for the meeting. I assume I'll have the same communications setup as before?"

"Of course," Gene told him.

"I have a question," Jim said, looking from Gene to Jackson. "Since you can hear everything, can you talk to me?"

Jackson looked at Gene and asked, "Can I?"

"I believe so," Gene answered. "If you don't already have the capability, you'll have it tomorrow.

Why do you ask?" he asked, looking at Jim.

"What if he offers a compromise?" Jim asked, looking at Jackson. "With only three days, you're shutting the door on other options. If he makes an offer and you believe it will accomplish your goals without sacrificing the man, couldn't you negotiate through me?

I'm not trying to get further involved, but it seems to me that he could keep asking for meetings, and the three days would expire," Jim added. "Then, your hands are essentially tied."

"You have a good point," Jackson told him, nodding. "Our goal is to get him out of office next term, not destroy him and blemish the office this term.

I'm amenable to some modification to the three-day mandate," he continued. "Let's just see where this takes us. If he doesn't come up with some acceptable solution, my silence is that it's unacceptable, and there will be no further negotiation. And there will be no further meetings.

Either he makes his announcement, or he'll be the next domino behind the congressman," Jackson said, turning to leave the room. "I'll see you tomorrow morning."

Chapter Forty-Six

At six o'clock the next morning, Jim had finished breakfast with Gene and was being transformed into Father Sarducci. "What do you think, General?" Jim asked as his robe was adjusted over his bulletproof vest. "Think I have a chance at becoming the head of some offshoot religion? Maybe emulating the Pentecostal?"

"I think not," he answered, laughing. "I've never been to one of their services, but I just can't see you getting jiggy like some of them reportedly do.

I couldn't even imagine you living in a monastery with a bunch of reclusive monks," Gene continued, shaking his head. "First off, you like women too much. Second, piousness is not your strong suit. And neither is being humble. No, you're exactly where you fit.

You've got the glamour of being an airline pilot and the adventurousness of doing what you do best," Gene concluded.

"And just what is it that I do best?" Jim asked as the final touches were made to his makeup.

"Eliminating," Gene answered. "Eliminating with impunity. Controlled and calculating. Focused would be a good description. But you're an instrument of death. Like it or not, that's your niche in the world where someone is tasked with ridding the world of those that prey on the innocent and helpless."

"You make it sound like I'm some vengeful demon," Jim complained.

"Not vengeful, though you can be," Gene argued. "You can be very compassionate … or cold and calculating when necessary. A rare breed, but people like you have been necessary throughout history."

Jim looked in the mirror and responded, "I'm the black knight charging into battle with evil. Is that what you're saying?"

"Maybe a white knight," Gene said, checking his watch. "And now it's time to go face the evil, Sir Knight. Your chariot awaits."

As they headed out, Jackson came in saying, "I just heard from a colleague who told me the President did ask someone within his security detail to do a little manipulation of the duty logs.

Good thing we beat him to it," he continued as he nodded his approval of Jim's transformation. "And I had the unredacted logs stamped and signed by the duty officer. Good suggestion, Jim."

"I'm sure you'd have thought of it yourself," Jim said as he checked the communications with his earpiece. "I may even get a chance to use that tidbit of information during our meeting."

"We've got to get you there for you to use it," Gene told them. "Your driver is waiting. The Senator and I will be monitoring you, as will the team that's already in place."

"I'm as ready as I'll ever be," Jim announced. "Let's hope that the gentleman and I use the term rather loosely, has finally come to the conclusion that his options are becoming as few as hen's teeth."

"One would hope," Gene said as they followed him out of the building. "But so far, the man considers himself bulletproof. Your job is to convince him otherwise."

As they approached the Suburban that would take Jim to the meeting, a man wearing a sports coat and khaki pants hurried to intercept them, saying, "Senator, I have an urgent message for you."

As Jackson took the message and read it, he said, "Looks like our man is still unwilling to play by the rules. I'm not positive, but it appears that he's sent a couple of men to the parlor.

They just arrived in a white Chevrolet van and are parked about halfway down the block," he added, showing Gene the note.

Gene quickly read the note and turned slightly, asking, "Blue Bell, are you in position?"

Hearing the team was, he told them, "White Chevy van, parked down the street. Two unknowns. Check it out."

"Let me know what's happening when you can," Jim said, getting in the Suburban. "If I don't hear from you before I get there, I'm going to remain in the car until you give me the all-clear."

"That's the best approach," Gene agreed. "It's possible that the President is unaware, sort of like the first visit, but we should assume that they aren't there for the ice cream.

Regardless, we'll encourage them to find the nearest Baskin Robbins if all they want is ice cream," he concluded. "As you suggested, stay in the car until we sort it out."

Chapter Forty-Seven

Jim was about halfway to the parlor when Gene spoke from where they were monitoring the operation, "The two guys from the van are on their way to our facility here. They didn't want to cooperate there, so we removed the problem."

"Let me know who sent them," Jim replied. "If they are from who I think sent them, it would be a nice card to hold if things don't go well during the meeting."

"Certainly," Gene told him.

A few minutes later, as they arrived at the parlor, Gene said, "Harry sent them, but we don't know if he acted alone or with his father's blessing."

"Got it," Jim replied, getting out of the car. "Are our two guys standing by?"

"They're just around the corner," Gene answered. "I'll send them your way if you think you need them. Just say, 'What the hell is going on?' and I'll have them stage some confrontation outside."

"Got it," Jim said, entering the parlor and stepping up to the counter. "Cup of Rocky Road, please."

Taking his ice cream and spoon to the same table, he glanced around the room to see if there had been any changes. Seeing nothing out of place, he started eating.

Moments later, the same agent he had seen last time entered and looked in his direction. Motioning for Jim to stand up, he nodded to another man standing just outside the door.

"Hands up, please," the second man said as he approached Jim. "You know the drill."

"He's clean," he told the guy at the door after a quick pat down.

"Check under the table," the first agent ordered.

Bending over and looking, he stood up and said, "Clean. Not even a cobweb."

"May I sit back down?" Jim asked with his hands still up. "I'd like to at least have another couple of bites of my ice cream before your boss comes in."

"Sit down," the agent said. "Just keep your hands in view from this point on until I leave."

With less than half of the bowl eaten, Jim stood as the President entered the room. Waiting until he took his seat, he sat down and said, "Would you like some ice cream, sir?"

"No," the President said. "I'd like to conclude this business and get back to what the people of the country elected me to do.

Is your organization willing to give me the week I asked for before announcing my retirement at the end of this term?" he asked.

Jim pushed the bowl away and answered, "My organization rejected it. However, they are willing to give you three days. Today is day one. If you fail to make the announcement by midnight of day three, the information will be released in its entirety to every news media and social network.

Just to keep the record straight, you did not ask for a week; you demanded it," Jim said, staring at the President. "My organization does not want to destroy your presidency. Nor did we want to destroy the careers and possibly families of the two we've exposed.

But the continued debauchery involving the Barco Do Amor is going to be stopped," Jim continued. "Even with just two men being exposed, the news media is starting to ask about a list of other men who took a cruise.

We could release the list and let the chips fall where they may," Jim continued. "But you talked about an impact … I can assure you that the impact would be global in nature. Our goal has been and will continue to be, to have every individual in our government who's on the list to leave public office. Those in the private sector can be dealt with by their companies.

We don't care what you do with your lives after that," Jim said, shaking his head. "But if any of you decide to attempt to remain in office beyond what we negotiate, that individual will be publicly disgraced."

"You still can't prove I was ever there," the President said, leaning forward menacingly. "I have proof that I was elsewhere."

Jim smiled slightly, leaned back, and replied, "We're aware of you having the Secret Service logs revised. Unfortunately for you, we had copies made and stamped with the date and time along with the signature of the duty officer before your men made the revision.

We also have two men who strangely wanted ice cream early this morning," Jim continued. "You might want to have one of your security team get their van when you leave. It's parked just down the street. I'm sure they'll recognize it.

Sir, the offer of three days is as generous as it's going to get," Jim told him after a short pause. "I don't know any other way to demonstrate to you that the Children of El Barco is serious. If the first two releases don't convince you of just how serious we are, I guess the only way to do so would be to release your information immediately after this meeting.

The choice is yours, sir," Jim concluded. "What's your answer?"

Chapter Forty-Eight

The President stared at Jim for a few seconds and then said, "You know, I've committed no crime. Even if what you say you can prove, it didn't happen here, and I can't be charged."

"Wrong, sir," Jim quickly responded. "True, the videos can't be placed on US soil where sex with underage children is a crime. However, the very act of paying underage children for sexual acts is a crime, and that happened on US soil. The very act of boarding the boat with those children happened on US soil.

And speaking of crime, we discovered a private aircraft belonging to one of your companies, the same LLC that paid for the excursion, brought you to Honolulu," Jim told him. "That aircraft, tail number N167BP, was traced back to where both you and your son boarded it.

Flight records from the FAA verify it left the Baltimore/Washington National airport, stopped to refuel in Orange County, and then continued to Honolulu," Jim said. "Now, as an aside, we looked into the company to verify your connection and determined that the LLC recently received a government bid to do some reconstruction on a Caribbean Island that was devastated by a hurricane.

Although your company's bid was the highest, it was awarded the contract over two lower bids," Jim said. "Then your LLC subcontracted the work to the company that had placed the lowest bid. You profited almost two million dollars.

Having said that, we don't care about what you and your family do," Jim said. "That's an issue for other entities. We're only concerned with your activities on the Barco Do Amor.

And regarding the unfortunate incident during our first meeting," he continued. "That's not a factor in this negotiating. Neither are the two gentlemen that were waiting for my arrival this morning."

"I had nothing to do with either of those," the President exclaimed.

"Doesn't matter," Jim interjected. "Those parties are being dealt with. This concerns only one issue … your announcement that you don't intend to run for another term. And it's got to be issued within the three days as previously discussed."

The President looked around for a few seconds and then offered, "What if I provided you with a letter of intent? Stating I won't be seeking a second term due to personal reasons. Would that be satisfactory?"

Jim sat quietly as he listened to Jackson tell him the conditions required and then answered, "Any such letter must be witnessed by three people: the Chief Justice of the Supreme Court, your Vice President, and the current Speaker of the House.

Additionally, it must be videoed," Jim added. "The letter must be provided within the same three-day window along with a copy of the video.

Once we have that, you have until the first of June of next year to make your formal announcement," Jim told him. "If we do not have the letter and video before midnight, as mentioned before, the material will be released.

And, if you do not publicly announce your decision to not seek a second term by the first of June next year, the material will be released," Jim continued. "And you should understand that this is the final offer.

Either you accept it right now, or you will be joining the first two gentlemen on the news this evening," Jim concluded. "For right now, your word is sufficient. But, you renege, and we'll expose you as we did the others. What's your answer?"

"What about your knowledge of the LLC issue? Will that be forgotten?" the President asked.

"My company will not pursue it," Jim replied, nodding.

"Then I'll accept your offer," he begrudgingly agreed. "But there will be no release of the letter of intent or the video. That's a deal breaker."

"We accept that condition," Jim answered, smiling slightly. "Why would we want to use a fly swatter when we have a cannon? All that letter does is buy you a few more months."

The President abruptly slid his chair back and stood, saying, "This is the last I hope to see of you … or any other member of your so-called organization."

As he turned to leave, the agent at the door checked outside, nodded at the President, and told Jim, "You know the drill. You stay in your seat with your hands in view until I leave. Understood?"

Jim merely nodded and looked at the now-melted ice cream.

Chapter Forty-Nine

Thirty minutes later, when Jim joined Gene and Jackson in the room where Jim was to have his wardrobe and makeup removed, he asked, "What do you think he's going to do?"

"Oh, I think he'll do as he agreed," Jackson said. "The stakes are too high for him to risk not doing so. Especially since he understands how much knowledge we possess about his lucrative side businesses."

"Yeah, he was a little surprised when I mentioned that," Jim said as the latex was pulled from his face. "I'd almost guess that he's more worried about his and his family's various enterprises than some indiscretions that he's probably indulged in on previous occasions.

Not that it's any of my business, but just how many of these LLCs does he have?" Jim asked as the last of the makeup was wiped from his face.

"We've uncovered at least fifteen," Jackson answered. "Some registered to him and a grandchild, some to him and an uncle or a brother. The only common thread is his name on the company board."

"I'm a little surprised that you agreed not to pursue that issue," Gene remarked as Jim rose from the chair and checked his appearance in the mirror.

"I only said my company won't pursue it," Jim replied, smiling. "I never agreed to the issue not being pursued by any other entity ... such as some government oversight committee."

"I'm not sure he'll see it that way," Gene argued as they headed out of the room. "He's under the impression that the issue is resolved with no repercussions to him or his family."

"Well, then he'd be wrong, wouldn't he?" Jackson replied. "Jim's correct. The company, neither Black Water nor the fictitious Children of El Barco, will pursue it.

It's about time someone used a technicality to mislead him after all of the times he's wordsmithed his way out of a statement or promise," Jackson added. "But the main goal has been achieved. He'll remain in office through this term, and we don't have to deal with the carnage that would result if we had to reveal his participation in underage child abuse.

And we avoid having that incompetent cackling hen of a Vice President leading the country," he finished. "All in all, I'd say we got the best result we could expect given the situation."

"What if he signs the letters as you required and then reneges when the elections approach?" Gene asked.

"I'm pretty sure he'll be in a more cooperative mood after we release the rest of the group," Jackson answered. "Not to mention a few leaks regarding those fifteen LLCs we know about.

Even if he tries to run for a reelection, I'm sure revealing the corruption will stymie his chances," he added. "Not to mention the publicity that's about to hit the news regarding the so-called list of participants of the Love Boat."

"Is that leaking already?" Jim asked as they returned to the briefing room where they had started that morning.

"Just a dribble for now," Jackson answered. "But the next public figure's retirement will put another crack in the dam. Toss in a tidbit regarding some of Britain's royal family, and the clamor for a release of the complete list will grow to a resounding crescendo."

"Who's the next on the list?" Gene asked.

"A junior Texas Congressman," Jackson told him. "Since he's started his second year, he'll need to be dealt with before he announces his bid for a second term."

"When do you want Jim to make him an offer he can't refuse?" Gene asked.

"This week," Jackson replied. "I want a couple of more political revelations so that word will spread within their circle that anyone who took a cruise on the Barco Do Amor is most likely going to have their names tossed to the press.

Then we'll sit back and watch the feeding frenzy begin," he concluded with a slight smile. "If you've ever wanted to watch people distance themselves from a contagious situation, you'll see it each time a new member of congress, or a corporation, suddenly has personal issues that require them stepping down."

"Then I guess I'm not needed here any longer," Jim responded, looking from Jackson to Gene. "I'll let Marie know that I'll be home this afternoon if that's all right with both of you."

"The plane is ready as we speak," Gene told him. "I ordered it to stand by as soon as Jackson told me about the next target. And, if it's not a problem, I'd like to come with you.

We can discuss the initial approach with your Texas representative as we head to Dallas," he added. "Not to mention, I'd enjoy some fine Italian cuisine if you know a reputable restaurant."

"I'll check to see if we can get reservations at a little family bistro just a few miles from where I live," Jim said. "Looks like the three days I had off due to being removed from a trip just became three days I'm going to be Father Sarducci."

"Only one of the three days," Gene corrected him, smiling at Jackson. "You can be your normal semiretired bum the other days. And just so you know, the makeup folks will be traveling with us. But they aren't invited to our evening with Marie and her family."

"And just so you know, you're only invited to tonight's dinner, not my evening with Marie," Jim said as they headed for the door. "And I'm hoping that the good Father won't be needed except for a single appearance."

"We all hope that's correct," Jackson added as they left. "And, with a little luck and publicity, the good Father's role will soon disappear."

"Is that good publicity or bad publicity?" Gene asked, following Jim down the hall.

"Is bacon good for breakfast?" Jackson responded as they reached the door to leave the building. "What's good for your breakfast may not be so good for the hog."

Chapter Fifty

Later that afternoon, as they were sitting with Marie at Siciliano's having a glass of wine while waiting for Marie's twin girls to arrive, she asked, "How did you get everything taken care of so quickly?

Just yesterday, you thought you'd be there for three or four days," she continued. "What happened?"

Gene looked at Jim and answered, "Our man Jim made a very persuasive argument."

"All I did was present the same thing you guys had presented before I met with the guy," Jim argued. "At most, I took your convoluted offer and simplified it. More or less, I dumbed it down to the lowest common denominator."

"What the inarticulate gentleman is trying to say is that he's a master at making a sow's ear out of a silk purse," Gene responded, laughing. "But, he's essentially correct. He broke the offer into segments, got agreements to the individual parts with minor modifications, and then to the entire package.

Goes back to the so-called Kiss Principle," Gene continued. "And if anyone can keep it simple, it's Jim."

"So, what are you planning for the next few days?" Marie asked Jim. "Now that you don't have to fly the trip you had and then a couple of days off after that, what's on your mind?"

"Whatever you plan, don't forget that we have a meeting with another client either tomorrow or the next day," Gene reminded him.

"I know," Jim said, nodding. "But I'll still have three or four days off after that before my next trip. I was thinking about taking a short drive up to where I grew up.

I haven't been there in a long time and wondered how much it has changed," he added, looking at Marie. "How'd you like a road trip?"

"Only if we take your truck," she answered. "I'm not sure I'd like sitting in that little Corvette of yours for more than a few minutes."

"Yeah, it's not the most comfortable car I've ever had," Jim agreed. "The pickup will definitely be better."

"Okay, so when do we leave?" she asked as her twins came into the room.

"Where are we going?" Seppa asked after kissing Marie on the cheek.

"You're going nowhere," Marie answered as Julie kissed her other cheek. "This is just Jim and I."

"Gemini?" Julie asked. "Isn't that a Zodiac sign? And it has something to do with twins."

"And we're twins," Seppa added. "So, if you're talking about Gemini, you must mean us!"

"Let me rephrase it for you," Marie said as they took seats around the table. "Me and Jim. I know that's grammatically incorrect, but it should remove any confusion regarding having you two going anywhere except back to school."

"Ah, now here's what I like to see," Anthony said, coming into the room. "Family and friends sitting around enjoying a glass of vino and talking."

"I don't have a glass of vino," Julie told him.

"Neither do I," Seppa chimed in.

Tony looked at Marie and asked, "Do you mean to deprive me of one of the few pleasures I have left in life? The pleasure of joining my grandchildren in a tiny glass of the nectar of the gods?"

"Okay, a tiny glass," Marie told them, laughing. "And only one."

Gene pulled his phone from his pocket and excused himself from the table as Marie poured two glasses, about a quarter of a normal glass of wine, saying, "And for you, Dad? Where's your glass?"

"I must have left it in the kitchen," Tony said, smiling at the girls. "I'll bring it when I come back."

"Then we get our tiny glass," Julie said, quickly swallowing her glass.

"Yeah, because it was supposed to be with Granddad," Seppa added as she finished hers. "This one didn't count."

As they continued arguing about whether or not they could have a refill, Gene motioned for Jim to come to the rear of the room.

Excusing himself, Jim walked back to where Gene was sitting at an empty table and waited for him to finish talking.

"He's right here," Gene said, looking up at Jim. "We can be wherever he wants to meet tomorrow afternoon."

Pausing while he listened, he then said, "We need a couple of hours for makeup and communication checks with Quantico and you. Set the meeting for two tomorrow afternoon if that will work for the Congressman."

After waiting for the response, Gene finished saying, "We'll call you in the morning to get the time and place. Also, any information you can gather before the meeting.

And not to bring up any potential problems, but do you anticipate anything like what happened on Jim's first meeting?" Gene asked.

"Good," Gene then said. "I'll look at it again when you let me know where the meeting is. Good evening."

Hanging up, Gene said, "Guess you heard enough to know that we'll be busy tomorrow morning and not sure how late, so it would probably be wise not to schedule anything with Marie until we see how the meeting goes."

"I'll take care of that," Jim said as Gene stood. "I don't think she really anticipated anything this evening, but I'll make sure she knows that I'll be going home alone. By the way, where are you staying?"

"The Embassy Suites, my home in Dallas," Gene answered as they walked back to where everyone was sitting. "The other folks are there also. I'll give you a call as soon I know when the meeting will be."

"Work again tomorrow?" Marie asked as they took their seats.

"Afraid so," Jim told her. "With some luck, I'll be free tomorrow afternoon. If you've no other plans, how about pizza and a movie at my house?"

Chapter Fifty-One

At ten o'clock the next morning, Jim pulled into the parking lot at the Embassy Suites to start the makeup procedure. Heading up to Gene's room, he wondered just how many more times he would be required to portray the good Father.

Gene answered the door as soon as Jim knocked and said, "Come on in. I just talked to the makeup folks, and we're heading downstairs for a quick lunch. Care to join us?"

"I'd rather go elsewhere, but sure, why not?" Jim answered. "How's the menu?"

"Nothing spectacular," Gene answered, pulling the door closed behind them. "But it beats goat's head gruel on a mountainside."

"Or fish head and rice in a jungle," Jim said as they knocked on another door.

"We're headed down," Gene told the guy who answered. "Pass the word. We'll start to work after we eat."

"Anything new?" Jim asked as they got in the elevator.

"Little background on our Congressman," Gene answered, pushing the button for the first floor. "Seems as if he had some issues when he was back in high school.

Now, remember, he was just seventeen," Gene told him. "But he had a rather unusual relationship with a fourteen-year-old friend of his sister."

"Think that's part of the reason for his passion for young girls?" Jim asked as the doors slid open.

"Could be," Gene replied, heading for the Tap and Grill. "There were a couple of complaints over the years but nothing that could be substantiated."

"Guess none of those matter," Jim said, heading for a large table. "What he's done lately, and we can prove is the only relevant issue. Will I have a chance to review the video and photos?"

"It's ready in my room when we get back," Gene said waving at two of the makeup team that walked in. "I don't think you'll need to see much of it to understand who you're dealing with."

"I just want to be able to tell the pervert that I've seen the videos," Jim said, taking a seat beside Gene. "And I bet you have a package to present to our little man, too."

"Right you are Grasshopper," Gene replied as the final men arrived. "Now, not to rush anyone, but we don't have too much time before Father Guido Sarducci meets the sinner and asks for his repentance. So, eat up, and we'll meet in my room in one hour."

Two hours later, as they were putting the finishing touches to the latex patches on Jim's face, he asked, "Where are we meeting?"

"You'll be meeting at the Dallas Fire Fighters Museum," Gene answered. "It's open to the public and can be fairly crowded.

I think he selected it because most of the people will be paying attention to the exhibits instead of two people sitting to the side," he finished. "Even if one of them looks like a medieval priest from a Monty Python movie."

"Will we have any security measures in place?" Jim asked as they began to blend the makeup to cover the latex and his normal skin tone.

"We've got a couple of men who will be wandering around with the crowd," Gene told him. "They'll have earpieces to listen to you in case you think you need assistance, but I can't imagine our guy being too aggressive.

My bet is that he'll come closer to bawling than brawling," Gene continued. "I wouldn't put it past him to have him pleading to make a deal. Anything that will make this go away."

"So, you think he'll take the deal we offer … announcing that he won't run for a second term?" Jim asked, donning the robe.

"Maybe not at first," Gene replied as they put Jim's Biretta on his head. "But given that we have the proof, and I'm sure he's heard about the CFO and the Congressman who have been publicly humiliated, I think he'll be easy to convince that that's his only graceful way out."

"Does he have children?" Jim asked, looking at himself in the full-length mirror.

"Two girls, ten and twelve," Gene said, knowing what Jim would say.

"I wonder what he'd think if some aged lothario was leering at his daughters?" Jim asked, turning to face Gene. "How can he even reconcile his acts with his family life?

And I won't even hint at anything even more repulsive," Jim said, shaking his head. "But the man's got problems, and I'm just the messenger, but I'm all in favor of dropping the hammer on this sorry piece of humanity.

Two daughters almost the same age as the ones he molested on the boat?" Jim questioned. "I'm not about to feel sorry for him. And if Jackson wants tact, I'm the wrong guy for this one."

"Speaking of that, let's get the communications with the Senator established," Gene said, ushering the makeup people out. "You can ask him about setting the rules when he's online with us."

Chapter Fifty-Two

An hour later, Jim was sitting on a bench across a wide aisle from where a group of children was looking at an old horse-drawn pumper painted a brilliant red with polished brass.

As the group was herded to the next exhibit, Jim saw the Congressman approaching. Rising, he waited until he was just a couple of feet away and said, "Congressman, please have a seat."

Waiting for him to sit, Jim sat down and handed him an envelope, saying, "I've been instructed to provide you with this information and let you look at it before we discuss the terms of the agreement."

As the Congressman took out the pictures one at a time and set them face down on the bench, he glanced up and down the now vacant aisle and asked, "Is this all?"

"Isn't that enough?" Jim asked incredulously.

"I don't see any crimes being committed," the Congressman said, replacing the photos in the envelope.

"Here we go again," Jim replied, shaking his head. "What happened on the boat is not technically a crime because it didn't happen on US territory or waters.

But the solicitation did," Jim explained. "You did pay for sex with underage females on US territory. You used the US banking system to transfer money. You used a US port to transport you and these children out past the twelve-mile limit with the purpose of sexual misconduct.

And before you start any further protest, you should look at the video, which shows you engaging in sexual activity within ten minutes of boarding the Barco Do Amor," Jim continued. "I'm not positive about how fast that boat is, but I sincerely doubt that it can do sixty miles an hour, and even then, you'd only be ten miles from port."

Jim paused for a couple of minutes, watching the Congressman slowly come to the realization that he wasn't going to escape the evidence he held in his hands. Finally, Jim asked, "What's your answer, sir?"

"I assume that you'll release this if I don't agree to announce my intentions to not seek a second term," he answered. "Does that preclude me from running for office later?"

"You've got to be shitting me," Jim exclaimed, shaking his head. "You think that this will disappear when you make a simple statement? Then you're free to run again? Or run for another office?

I'm here to make sure you understand the offer. The offer is that you announce you won't be running for a second term. I'm not authorized to make any modifications to that agreement. But I'm not restricted from telling you my position regarding your failure to accept the offer.

The company has given you thirty days to make the announcement," Jim told him. "You have thirty days. If you are as much as an hour late, I'm going to do everything within my power to make sure every graphic detail of your disgusting behavior is exposed.

And I'll personally make sure copies of the videos, photos, and records that prove incontrovertibly you molested children just a year or two older than your own to your wife and every family member I can uncover," Jim finished. "And trust me, I can find them all. Now, you have exactly one minute to give me your answer. At the end of that minute, if I don't have your agreement to make the announcement as directed, I'm going to request the immediate release of every sickening picture and the videos."

"You said I had thirty days to make the announcement," the Congressman protested. "And you said you aren't authorized to make any modifications."

"I lied. Fifty seconds," Jim said, staring at him.

"This is blackmail," the Congressman said.

"Forty seconds," Jim said.

"How do I know you have the authority to do this?" the Congressman asked, glancing around nervously.

"Thirty seconds," Jim said.

"Okay, okay," the Congressman finally said, dropping his head. "I'll make the announcement. Are you satisfied?"

"No, I'm not satisfied," Jim said, standing. "If it was left to me, I'd have already exposed you for the sick pervert you are.

But it's not left to me," Jim continued. "And even though you've agreed to the company's terms, I'd give the evidence to your wife. At least she'd have a warning that you might try the same shit with your own daughters."

"You can't do that," the Congressman said, standing with the envelope in his hands. "You promised. You promised that this would never be released if I left office."

"Maybe I lied again," Jim said, looking directly at him. "Sometimes things just have a way of leaking out, even under the best of intentions.

And if you think back, you were only told that it wouldn't be released to the public," Jim told him as he turned away. "There was never a guarantee that it wouldn't be revealed to your family. You'll never know if it will be, but even a hint of this activity again could make that a reality.

Come get me away from this piece of shit," Jim quietly said to the people monitoring the meeting as he walked away. "I need to take a three-hour shower to wash away the filth I've had to sit by for the last hour."

Chapter Fifty-Three

"Pretty hard on the man," Jackson said as Jim got to the hotel room with Gene to debrief the meeting. "Are you letting this get personal?"

"Definitely," Jim answered as he took a seat at the oval table.

"I don't think anyone can see what this man did and not take it personally."

"What about the others?" Jackson asked. "Did you take the meetings with the President as personal?"

"No, I guess I didn't," Jim confessed. "But this one really bothered me. I think it was because I could imagine that pervert going into his daughters' bedroom and having the same thoughts about doing what he did on the boat."

"What about threatening him with telling his wife?" Jackson asked. "What was the point in that? You already had his agreement to announce he wouldn't run for office again, so why that? I mean, we had what we wanted. That should have been the end of it."

"I didn't exactly threaten him with telling his wife," Jim explained. "I said if it was up to me, I'd do it. Not that it would be."

"Then what was the point?" Jackson asked, pressing the issue.

"Maybe I just wanted the piece of shit to wonder if a package might show up on his doorstep someday while he's away," Jim answered. "Maybe I just want him to think about that every second of every day.

I know we got what we wanted," Jim continued. "But I wanted him to think about what would happen to his life if his family ever found out. Maybe part of it was when he asked if he could run again after not running for reelection this time. It seemed as if he wasn't worried about what he had done, just how long he would have to wait until he could resume his old life. And by his old life, I'm including his fixation with little girls."

The room was quiet for several seconds, then Gene asked, "Do you think you'll have any issues with any of the others? By that, I'm asking if you can stick to the purpose of why we're doing this."

Jim sat back and closed his eyes for a couple of seconds and then answered, "Yeah. And I apologize for pushing the gentleman as far as I did. It won't happen again."

Gene looked at Jim for a second and then asked the Senator, "Are you satisfied, or would you like to have Jim replaced?"

"No, I don't want him replaced," Jackson quickly answered. "And to be honest, I'm not so sure I wouldn't have done the same thing if I had been sitting there face to face with that man.

Yes, our objective is to remove these folks from office, either political office or otherwise," Jackson continued. "As long as we accomplish that, I'm satisfied.

Along that vein, I was just told that some reporter for the Washington Post ran an article mentioning the Barco Do

Amor," Jackson told them. "It seems as if there's a minor clamor for the list of those people's names."

"Do you plan on releasing it?" Gene asked.

"Definitely not," Jackson replied, shaking his head. "Some of those people didn't participate in anything illegal or immoral. Some were just there for some time at sea with their wives, girlfriends, or maybe like the President's son, some pharmaceuticals, and a couple of close female companions.

No, releasing the entire list wouldn't benefit anyone and do harm to some innocent folks," he finished. "And I'm not interested in what those people from England or Ireland or Pakistan did. The original objective was to take care of our problems. Let the others take care of theirs if they're so inclined."

"Who's next?" Jim asked. "And when do you want me to make the meeting?"

"I think giving the press a couple of days to leak the information will do us some good," Jackson answered. "I'm hoping that when the name of the boat and its connection to those people who have already lost their positions becomes public knowledge, the other clientele will be a little more amenable to just a phone call.

Maybe Father Sarducci won't be required to convince them that an early retirement is their best choice," Jackson continued. "Hopefully, just a note from the Brazilian Embassy will suffice. Hopefully. Now, gentlemen, I have to go."

As soon as the Senator hung up, Jim asked, "When are you going to shut down the operation in Brazil?"

"A week after we close the operation in Honolulu," Gene answered. "And we're setting that up for one week from today."

"Won't losing their boat in Honolulu alert them to a problem?" Jim asked.

"Of course," Gene answered. "But they have other boats in other countries. Some just river cruises, others floating casinos with special accommodations. They will continue to operate as normal until we hit."

"What about those other operations?" Jim asked. "What will happen there?"

"Information regarding them will be passed to the country with jurisdiction," Gene answered. "Then it will be up to them to take care of their problem."

"Have there been US citizens using those boats?" Jim asked, knowing there most likely was.

"Of course," Gene explained. "But none of the patrons have used US-based facilities, such as our banks, and none of them are on the Senator's list. So, the information will be passed and that's all we're contracted to do. Let's not get over our heads here. The vast majority of the folks using the overseas facilities are not US citizens.

And I've been assured that the lists from those operations will be made public once the Brazilian operation is closed," Gene said as he headed for the door. "Now, let's get started on your role as one of the happy couples that will be taking your friends on a group conjugal cruise."

Chapter Fifty-Four

"What's the main objective of the operation?" Jim asked. "Is it to sink the ship or kill the crew?"

"Both," Gene answered. "The crew is as culpable as the head of the organization back in Brazil. If we're going to dismantle this organization, it means we don't make distinctions between the bottom and the top. They all have to go."

"What about one of the crew that has no clue about what the purpose of the boat actually is?" Jim asked. "I think it might be going a little too far to just eliminate anyone who happens to be working as, let's say, a Steward."

"I can guarantee you that everyone on that boat knows exactly what's going on," Gene argued. "First, let's take a look at how those crew members are selected. Number one, they have some family connections. Number two, they know that if they were to ever discuss who was doing what, their lives would be over. Those people pulled every string they could to get those positions. The fact that most of them have been working for the company for years tells you everything you need to know about how involved they are.

Let's compare their role to the role of the crew who operated Maria's Fortune out of Galveston," Gene said. "And the boat from Mexico that met them at sea. We sent two boats to the bottom of the Gulf of Mexico. And the crews were just like these on the Love Boat.

They all knew what the operation was and elected to participate because of the monetary reward. Let's not start splitting hairs about who lives and who dies. We could spend a lifetime trying to justify our actions. All we can do is have one rule … any involvement is evidence of complicity in every aspect of the operation.

And the degree of complicity is irrelevant," he finished. "If the crew members didn't want to be involved, they wouldn't have gone to the effort they did to get the jobs. No, they suffer the same fate as their bosses back in Brazil."

"Understood," Jim replied, nodding. "Now, the question becomes, do we eliminate them prior to sinking the boat, or do we let them go down with the boat and drown."

"Let's look at the first option, eliminate them, and then sink the boat," Gene answered. "There'll be no doubt as to the outcome. You'll have absolute proof that the mission is accomplished. Especially when the explosion occurs, and the boat disappears beneath the waves.

In the second option, you can never be sure that everyone perished,' he continued. "Let's say that the Captain survives and manages to send a message that results in a rescue operation. Possibly more than one person survives.

That is a likely scenario since they stay close to the shore and twelve to fifteen miles is normal," Gene explained. "So, the boat goes down, but there are survivors. Those survivors might possibly be able to identify any of you and your team.

That identification gets tied back to Father Sarducci," he continued. "That possibly leads to our Senator. None of this is necessary if we just make sure there are no survivors."

"Understood," Jim replied. "Now, have you planned how six people are going to overcome ten? And from what I've read, a yacht of that size can have a crew of over twenty."

"True enough," Gene replied. "But, since there will only be three cabins occupied and there have been no special cabin attendants requested, ten is the number they normally go to sea with.

There's always the Captain, an Engineer with possibly an assistant, a Mate or two, enough Stewards to take care of the passengers and crew, and the Chef," Gene explained. "We've analyzed each cruise for the last couple of years, and we expect ten.

If there's a change to that once you board the ship, you'll have to make adjustments," he finished. "Even if there are a couple more people, that shouldn't change the operation."

"Have you decided how to deploy our folks?" Jim asked, thinking about who would be handling which members.

"Yes, you'll have the Captain and the Engineer," Gene answered. "It's vital that both of them be removed before anyone can send a distress signal.

Your partner will be responsible for the Steward that serves your cabin," he continued. "And the other ladies will do the same.

One of the *husbands* will take care of the Chef and any kitchen staff," he explained. "And the other one will be responsible for the Mate and any assistant.

Now, having said that, you'll be responsible for how these people manage their assignments," Gene continued. "If we plan on executing the operation the morning after you put to sea, we believe that you can expect the Captain and

Engineer to be having breakfast an hour or so before your standing request for what time you're served breakfast.

There's nothing out of the ordinary for a guest to wander into the dining room before scheduled meals," Gene explained. "So, if you can remove those two at that time, it simplifies the operation. And, since a meal is being served, the Chef and a Steward or two should be in the kitchen.

That leaves the Mate and an assistant or two for the other husband," Gene finished. "Toss in the three Stewards who will be dispatched by the cabin occupants, and you've got six people to round up any remaining crew."

"What's that old saying about the best-laid plans?" Jim remarked, shaking his head. "You make it sound so simple. But the reality is seldom so simple."

"Remember Occam's Razor," Gene responded, handing Jim a schematic of the yacht. "The simplest answer is usually the correct one. But prior preparation prevents piss poor performance, so here's the layout of the Love Boat for you to study in your spare time. And we're going to have a little get-together with the entire crew later this week to make sure everyone is on the same page."

"And then you're going to tell me that flexibility is the key to success," Jim said, standing and taking the brochure. "And lack of information is the key to flexibility. Therefore, the less I know, the more likely I'll be successful."

"Guess that's one way of looking at it," Gene said as they left the hotel room. "Now, I'm going to get the makeup folks back to Quantico. Tell Marie I'm sorry that I didn't get a chance to come for dinner again and say goodbye, but duty calls."

"I'll take care of it," Jim said, heading for the elevators. "Maybe I can actually do my primary job before *duty* calls me again. You know, fly airplanes."

Chapter Fifty-Five

Later that evening, as Jim and Marie were sitting in his living room watching *The Big Lebowski*, she hit pause on the remote and asked, "How did your meeting go this morning?"

"No problems," Jim answered, looking at her. "The gentleman involved understood the issues we were having and agreed to make revisions to his long-range goals to implement our requests."

"That's a long answer that really doesn't provide much of an answer," she said, leaning back and crossing her arms.

Jim turned slightly and then said, "Marie, I can't discuss much of what I do with Gene and his company. I'm sure you understand that since you had to deal with it before your husband was shot.

There are always going to be things that I can't talk about," he continued. "It's not that I don't trust you or want you to understand what I'm doing, but you have to let me decide what I can discuss and what I can't."

"Does this company Gene works for… Black Water, I think you told me. Do they do any sort of clandestine operations?" she asked, watching his face.

"Depends on what you mean by clandestine," Jim answered. "If you meant it to mean secret operations, then yes. But I'm sure you were familiar with undercover officers, and that's also clandestine operations, isn't it?"

"Okay, how about does the company do anything like assassinations?" she then countered.

"Then I'd say no," Jim responded, shaking his head. "But that's not to say that there aren't situations when the company's men aren't required to defend themselves.

That's true of any security detail," he explained. "Take the Secret Service that provides security for the President. I'm sure they've had to shoot people that were trying to harm the President.

Same for one of our people assigned to provide security for a visiting dignitary," he continued. "If either he feels threatened or his assignee is, then he's free to respond. I guess you could call that assassination if you want."

"No, that's not what I'm asking," Marie replied. "I'm asking specifically if the company is ever hired to assassinate a specific individual, like the man who murdered David."

"Not that I know of," Jim answered, looking directly into her eyes. "Now, there are areas of the company that I'm not allowed to know about, but I don't personally know if the company has ever assassinated someone. Why do you ask?"

"It's just something I've been wondering about since it seemed so coincidental that shortly after I met you and Gene, the police department suddenly finds the guy who shot David, and he just happened to have been shot by some white supremacist guy," she continued. "After the police have been looking for over two years, you and Gene show up, and suddenly, they find the man. Don't you find that to be just a little bit of a coincidence?"

"No," Jim answered, shaking his head. "How would I know who shot David? How would Gene or the company know who did it? I think you're adding one and one and one and coming up with five.

I don't know, but I'm sure if you asked the Dallas Police Department, they'll let you know how they discovered the man who shot David and that it had nothing to do with either Gene, me, or Black Water," he continued. "Of course, if it was one of their undercover officers, they wouldn't be able to tell you either.

I've been working for Black Water for almost ten years," Jim then told her. "I've been assigned to some strange contracts, but I've never been sent to kill anyone. And most of my experience is with facility security and personal protection.

And I've known Gene for over twenty years, and I'd be willing to bet that he's never been asked to kill someone," Jim finished. "Just because someone's dog attacks someone during a full moon doesn't make the dog a werewolf. But if you want to question Gene about it, please do."

Marie picked up the remote and paused before saying, "I'll take your word for it. Maybe I've got a curiosity streak that's wider than normal, but after so many times you leave for two or three days and you never tell me why, I just wonder why you don't?"

"First, most of our contracts are confidential," Jim told her. "We're prevented from discussing security measures with anyone not directly involved. If a breach of one of our security contracts were to ever occur, that could cost the company untold millions of dollars, if not more. Especially if that resulted in someone gaining classified information that damaged the company. Or in the death of one of our upcoming assignees for security.

I wish I could tell you more, but just think how I'd feel if what I told you was what got someone hurt," he finished. "And you'd never believe how boring ninety percent of the assignments are. Standing outside a closed door while a meeting is taking place. Pouring over architectural plans for an embassy. Not quite James Bond thriller stuff."

"So, I guess no black-tie affairs in exotic places for me then?" she joked as she hit the play button. "I guess it can't be too secret since you did invite me to come to Washington just a few days ago while you were working."

Chapter Fifty-Six

Jim had just gotten home from a three-day trip with American when Gene called.

"How'd the trip go?" Gene asked.

"Horrible," Jim answered as he placed his suitcase on the bed. "The Captain was a real pain in the ass. I was worried that one of the Flight Attendants was going to put Visine in his coffee."

"What was so bad about him?" Gene asked.

"Basically, he thought he had to tell each member of the crew how to do their jobs every leg," Jim told him as he pulled the dirty clothes from his suitcase. "And, of course, everyone had to address him as *Captain*. Lord knows you couldn't use his first name."

"What was his background?" Gene asked.

"Commuter pilot," Jim said, putting fresh socks and underwear in the suitcase.

"No military experience?" Gene asked.

"Nope," Jim responded, putting his uniform in the closet. "But I've flown with pure civilian pilots before, and they've been great guys to fly with. This guy just has some insecurity complex. And not to mention, he couldn't fly for shit. Add to that, he was a chunky monkey.

I was worried that one of the buttons on his shirt would pop off and hit someone in the eye," Jim continued as he pulled on a pair of Wrangler jeans and a T-shirt. "Reminded me of Wimpy, the fat character in the Popeye movie who said, 'I'll gladly pay you Tuesday for a hamburger today'. So, all together, it made for a horrible trip," Jim finished heading for the kitchen.

"Now, what's on your mind? I'm sure you didn't call just to discuss my experiences with the outside world."

"Now that hurts. Really, can't I just call an old friend and ask how his life's going?" Gene replied, chuckling. "But, since you are in such a pissy mood today, I'll get to the business at hand.

I brought the Honolulu team down last night," he explained. "We're all in the Crowne Plaza on Stemmons Freeway. If it would fit your schedule, we'd enjoy your attendance at a little simulation of the upcoming mission. Think you can fit us in?"

"Let me check with my personal assistant," Jim said, grabbing a Ziegen Bock from the refrigerator. "Looks like I can squeeze you in between a photo shoot for America's most handsome pilot at noon today and a black-tie dinner with the Mayor this evening at eight o'clock."

"I think that'll work for us," Gene replied. "Since the photo shoot will probably last about thirty seconds in your imagination, and I happen to know the Mayor is in Austin meeting with the Governor. How about meeting me at Cantina LAREDO in an hour and we'll have a late lunch before heading back to the hotel?"

"Guess I can make the necessary alterations to my schedule," Jim replied, taking a sip of his beer. "Am I to assume that I'll be introduced to my lovely bride at that point?"

"She can hardly wait," Gene answered, laughing. "She made some remark after seeing your picture on the briefing package and asked, 'What does any woman find attractive about this guy?'"

"And why didn't I get a briefing package?" Jim asked, seeing that he needed to finish his beer and get on the road to make it to the restaurant on time.

"Yours is in my room," Gene answered. "I'd have sent it to you earlier, but I was worried that you might develop some incurable disease after seeing your bride's picture."

"Guess we can't all be roses," Jim responded, tossing his empty bottle in the trash can. "Someone has to be the dandelion in the flowerbed. I mean, how do we get so many ugly people if it wasn't for ugly people getting together?"

"Alcohol?" Gene answered, laughing. "See you at the restaurant. And no one in the team knows anything about Father Sarducci or that part of the operation. They're only involved in this piece of it."

"No problem," Jim replied, heading for the garage. "By the way, I'll bring the 'Vette, and my bride can ride with me back to the hotel. Maybe she'll have a different opinion of me when she sees what a classy guy I must be to have such a classy car."

"Drive the truck," Gene advised. "I'm not sure she can fit in the 'Vette, and even your half-ton pickup may be pushed to the limit."

"You're such an ass, sir," Jim said, laughing, starting the car. "But I'm pretty sure you picked the right lady to pretend to be my wife, or that could jeopardize the mission. These folks are used to the glamour crowd, and we've got to fit their expectations."

Chapter Fifty-Seven

Following Gene back to the Crowne Plaza, Jim followed him to his room and met the rest of the team, who were gathered around a model of the yacht they would be spending the night on.

"Jim, this is your blushing bride for one night, Mischelle," Gene started introducing everyone. "And this is Larry, whose wife of the night is Carolyn. And finally, Rob, whose wife is Becky. Folks, meet Jim."

After shaking everyone's hand, Jim glanced at the mockup of the yacht and asked, "How accurate is this model?"

"Pretty much one hundred percent," Gene answered as everyone gathered around the table. "We looked at every variation of the ship and verified it with our guys who've been working on it when it's inshore.

There are a couple of additions, such as a locker in the Captain's quarters that contains the firearms," Gene continued as he removed the top layer of the model to reveal the cabins. "That's about the only modification to the basic design."

"Who has access to the locker?" Jim asked, looking at the minor details of the model.

"The Captain, of course, the Mate, and the Engineer," Gene replied. "None of the other crew members are authorized to be armed."

"Does anyone normally carry a sidearm?" Jim asked.

"Not normally," Gene explained, replacing the top of the model. "Our best guess is that you six will be the only armed people on the yacht.

And if you just happen to enter the dining room half an hour early, you shouldn't have any difficulty taking care of the Captain and the Mate," he finished.

"What about if any of the kitchen staff is there?" Jim asked, looking at Rob, who was responsible for the Chef.

"Shoot them," Gene replied. "Rob will be taking care of anyone else who's in the kitchen at the same time, and that could include any of the yacht's crew. Since your weapons will be silenced, no one else should be alerted regardless of where they are."

"Where will the Mate be?" Larry asked, trying to figure out where he needed to be when the action started.

"He'll probably be on the bridge," Gene answered, pointing to the location on the model. "He's basically just monitoring the boat until the Captain or Engineer relieves him. Since you'll be anchored, there isn't much to do until time to return to shore."

"When will the stewards come to our cabins?" Mischelle, the lady playing Jim's wife, asked.

"Normally, not until you go to breakfast," Gene told her. "There's a phone that connects the cabins to the bridge, so if you call and say you'd like to have all three cabins cleaned as the guys leave, the stewards should be there while the guys are taking care of their people.

One other thing that you'll be using is the communication system on your phones," he told them, looking at each one. "When we get to Honolulu, we'll make sure every phone is connected through the satellite, and we can monitor you as well as tell you exactly where everyone is. If anyone has any problems, just say what you need, and Jim can assign any one of you to help."

"What about the Mate's assistant?" Larry asked. "Will he be on the bridge?"

"Normally not," Gene answered. "But he could be there if the Mate needs him. "Most likely, he'll be in his cabin or in the kitchen. Your primary target is the Mate.

There may well be some people that you'll have to hunt down," Gene explained. "What we're discussing is just an outline of how we believe the situation will be.

It's entirely possible that the Captain will be on the bridge with the Mate if there are any problems with the boat," he continued. "Possibly the Engineer also. But we're going to be monitoring everyone's location through the cameras we've had installed, and we'll update you that morning before you leave your cabins.

Jim will then make any adjustments to how you're deployed based on their actual locations," he told them. "Every one of you was selected for this operation because you've shown that you can adapt to a fluid and changing situation.

I expect the same here," he finished. "Jim will be the final authority on making changes or redirecting your assignments, and if you see something that's counter to what was expected, let him know. If we do this right, you can expect to be back on the island before noon."

"Which lifeboat will we be using?" Jim asked, looking at the location of two lifeboats on opposite sides of the yacht.

"The one on the port side," Gene answered, pointing to it. "The control for the davit system is located in the bow and electrically lowers the boat once you are all onboard."

"How long do you think we'll be waiting for you to come get us?" Kathy asked.

"Less than half an hour," Gene told her. "We'll have a boat leave the harbor when we hear the operation has started. It'll have your exact location based on the GPS coordinates, and if it's where we expect you to be, it shouldn't be much more than twenty minutes."

"What about our weapons?" Jim asked, trying to visualize the end of the operation. "I think we should toss them overboard once we're coming back."

"The Captain picking you up will take care of that," Gene answered. "They've located an area that divers don't visit due to a lack of coral reefs or other interesting sights. He'll drop them in a very narrow trench that's deeper than most amateur divers go anyway. Now, are there any other questions?"

"Only one," Jim answered, looking at the rest of the team. "When do we do this?"

"Seven days," Gene answered. "That means that you'll be heading to Honolulu the day you get back from your next trip. Everyone else will be here the night before, and we'll have a Gulfstream five at Love Field ready to go when you get there."

"Guess I better have another bag packed and in the truck," Jim said, shaking his head. "At least I'll have one day off before I have to go back to work with American. And I'll be doing laundry all day, so I'll have clean socks for that trip."

"You do lead an exotic life, my friend," Gene said as he headed for the door. "Just think of how many people would love to have the opportunity to travel as you do."

"And all of them would be as tired of living out of a suitcase as I am," Jim retorted, waiting for the rest of the team to leave the room.

Realizing that Jim wanted to talk in private, Gene shut the door as the last one left and asked, "Is there something else on your mind?"

Chapter Fifty-Eight

As Gene came over to where Jim was examining the model of the yacht, he asked again, "Is there something you want to talk about?"

Jim set the top of the model back in place and asked, "What's happening with the other part of this operation? Specifically with the President."

"He gave us the letter of intent, signed by the Chief Justice, the Vice President, and the Speaker of the House, just as we requested," Gene answered. "We also received the video. So basically, he's off the table until next June when he's sworn to announce he's not running."

"Of course, we all know that he'd renege at the drop of a hat if he thought he could," Jim argued. "And all I think we've done is to give him several months to concoct a plausible story."

"That's beyond our purview," Gene responded. "We've done what we were asked, and now we let that matter rest with the Senator. If the time comes when he wants something additional, we'll cross that bridge then."

Gene watched Jim for a couple of minutes and then said, "Somehow, I don't think that's what's really on your mind, is it?"

Jim sighed and told him, "No. There's an issue with what's going on with Marie."

"I thought you two were getting along great," Gene said, surprised at the revelation. "What's the issue?"

Pausing to gather his thoughts, Jim finally said, "Things are going great. But she's voiced some suspicions about my relationship with you and asked questions that I've had to lie about.

The problem is more that I don't like to lie to her," Jim admitted. "But I believe she needs to hear the truth about the risks involved.

Just like with Jennifer, she bore the risk without knowing about it," Jim continued. "She wouldn't have been killed except for her connection with me. She at least should have been given the opportunity to make that decision with full knowledge of that risk."

"You can't take the blame for that," Gene countered. "That had nothing to do with you personally. Just an unfortunate encounter."

"That's bullshit, and you know it," Jim replied, looking Gene in the eye. "I was targeted specifically because I work for Black Water. That fact hasn't changed. Who's going to be next targeting one of our people?

It's bad enough when we take the risk on the job, such as Jewell getting shot during the meeting," Jim continued. "But when we, meaning me, expose someone to that risk, I believe they should know."

"And what do you think Marie would do if she knew the full extent of your involvement?" Gene argued. "Do you think she'd run away? She faced the same issue when she married a cop, and she knew those risks."

"No, I don't think she'd leave," Jim replied. "But I think she deserves the opportunity to make that decision."

"Are you asking for my permission to tell her?" Gene asked after seeing the resolve in Jim's eyes.

"No, I'm not asking permission," Jim told him, shaking his head. "I'm telling you my intentions. If that's something the company can't condone, then I'll resign."

Gene paused before saying, "How much detail do you think Marie needs to know? And just as importantly, how do you think that knowledge would impact your relationship with her?"

"I'm not going to tell her about the specifics of any operation, past or future," Jim explained. "But she's already questioned the company's involvement in the elimination of her husband's killer.

The lady's no dummy," Jim continued. "And I can't keep lying to her. I just can't. And I won't. The only question is what the company decides is the boundary of revealing information regarding certain operations."

"First, let's dismiss any idea of your resignation," Gene said. "Look at it this way … Jennifer knew you were a Marine and were going back to Vietnam. Exactly what each mission involved wasn't discussed. All she knew was that you were an F4 pilot, and that the news certainly informed her that F4s dropped bombs and were occasionally shot down."

Pausing, Gene added, "Now, just how some of our operatives share some basic detail of their lives working for Black Water, I don't know. But I know you've had high-level security details before and never revealed them.

I don't see the difference here," Gene continued. "I don't see the harm in letting her know that you contract with Black Water. You've already admitted that except not the exact nature of your activities.

Finally, I think you're underestimating Marie," he finished. "I'm willing to bet that she'll take it in stride just as she did with her husband's career, just as Jennifer did when you went back to Vietnam.

Now, you do what you believe is necessary regarding Marie," Gene added. "I speak for the company, saying that I trust you to know how far to go involving her. The company, and more specifically, I, have trusted you for too many years to count, and you've always made the right decision. I expect nothing less from you now. So, no more thoughts about resigning."

"Done," Jim said, extending his hand for Gene to shake. "Now, if the company has no further need of me today, I'm going to take a certain special lady out to dinner. And, just to show you I can keep details from unauthorized disclosure, you'll never know what I'm ultimately planning for this evening."

Chapter Fifty-Nine

After getting back from dinner, Jim and Marie were sitting in the living room watching Blazing Saddles when Jim paused the movie and said, "I have a little confession to make."

Marie turned and looked at him for a second and then asked, "Just what's this about?"

"I want to clarify what we discussed the other day regarding my association with Gene and Black Water," he said, laying the remote on the arm of the couch.

Making sure he had her full attention, he continued, "What I told you was pretty much the truth, but the company does get involved in situations that require eliminating someone.

For example, when I was assigned to Dark Water, the enforcement arm of Black Water for international operations, I was sent to one of the countries in the Middle East where we were negotiating with one of the Tribal Chiefs," he explained. "I was there to deliver a package to a certain location upon receiving directions.

I was living on the side of a hill watching for an individual, who I did not know, to signal where I was supposed to leave the package," he continued. "I never knew what was in the package … either money to pay off the man or a bomb to eliminate him."

"Did you ever find out which it was?" Marie asked.

"No," Jim answered, shaking his head. "Once I left the package beside the building, I was removed and brought home. I never heard what happened after that."

"So, you don't know if you assassinated anyone," Marie argued.

"Not then," Jim confessed. "But I have been involved in operations where I was responsible for eliminating someone."

"Does this have anything to do with David?" she asked suddenly.

"The company did not have anything to do with that other than determine who shot him," Jim explained. "They used some facial recognition program that's far beyond what any other law enforcement or governmental branch currently has.

They identified the shooter to the Dallas Police Department and provided them with the evidence," he added. "What they did with the information, you'll have to ask them."

"So, I was right," Marie responded, nodding. "You and Gene were the reason why the guy was found. I knew there had to be some connection."

"That's not exactly true," Jim replied, shaking his head. "Gene got involved at my suggestion. I mentioned what had happened to David and asked if the company could assist the police in figuring out who had shot him.

Gene passed the request on to someone in the computer department that knows about the facial recognition program, and they developed the images that proved who the man was," he clarified. "The company was really never involved. There were no contracts, no financial issues, just assisting in solving a crime. And that was because Gene knew about the program and convinced the company to let him have access to it.

Now, you can say I was involved," Jim said. "I asked Gene for help in finding the shooter. Gene was involved because he asked the company. But the company was never involved in finding the man or in the circumstances surrounding his death. For the answer to those things, again, you'll have to ask the Dallas Police."

"Why does Black Water have computer programs that are so much better than what's available to the local police?" Marie asked after thinking about Jim's explanation. "If the company has something like that, why can't anyone use it?"

"It's something to do with patent laws," Jim answered. "The lady who developed the program works for the company, but she has the sole right to anything she develops. That was part of her contract when she joined the company. So, the program doesn't belong to the company; it belongs to her. And its use outside of the company is prohibited without her express approval."

"So, she just let the Dallas Police use her program?" Marie asked.

"Not exactly," Jim explained. "She took all of the images they had, fed them into the computer, and gave the Dallas Police the name that matched the results. She would never allow anyone to have access to the program because they may be able to copy it.

But she helped because she could and because a colleague asked her," Jim finished. "Now, she may have helped other departments, such as Homeland Security, or the FBI, or the CIA. But I don't know anything about that. All I can tell you is that she, not the company, helped find the guy that killed David. That's the extent of their involvement."

Marie sat looking at Jim for a minute and then finally said, "I guess if that's the extent of the company's involvement, I'd still like to thank them. And Gene."

"No thanks for me?" Jim asked, picking up the remote.

"I'll think of a way to thank you after the movie," she replied, smiling.

Chapter Sixty

The next morning, after Marie left, Jim was doing laundry and repacking his suitcase for the upcoming trip. He had just finished putting one load in the dryer and another in the washer when his phone rang.

"Hello," he said as he turned the dial and started the washing machine.

"Good morning, Jim," Gene said. "Sounds like you're being domestic this morning."

"Someone has to do it," Jim replied, smiling. "Unless the company wants to supply me with maid service, I guess it's up to me. What can I do for you this morning?"

"Nothing this morning," Gene answered. "But we have a minor problem that requires a certain Father Sarducci to make a visit."

"Who's not wanting to play ball?" Jim asked, heading for the kitchen.

"There's a certain City Councilman down there that doesn't believe that he needs to seek employment elsewhere," Gene told him.

"I'm guessing that he's been provided with evidence of his misdeeds," Jim responded, pouring a cup of coffee and putting it in the microwave.

"Of course," Gene answered. "His response was, 'I got better videos than that crap you sent me, and my constituents down here don't give a rat's ass what I do as long as I keep the Benjamins rolling in. Hell, you could have a two-hour movie of me with a flock of sheep wearing lace stockings and lipstick, and they'd probably buy a copy."

"What do you expect me to do?" Jim asked, taking the warm cup of coffee to the table on the porch. "Wasn't the plan to present the individual with the evidence and let them decide what to do? If he doesn't care about the fallout, why should we?"

"There's another issue here," Gene explained. "This gentleman seems to have gotten his hands on some of the names on the list and is threatening to release them to the press."

"How the hell did that happen?" Jim asked, surprised at the revelation.

"We're not exactly sure," Gene told him. "It's most likely that he knew about those individuals who resigned or left their position, like the Dallas preacher, and added two and two.

We've known all along that some of the people on the list knew about each other," Gene continued. "Matter of fact, that's how some of the individuals learned about the little operation."

"So, you want Guido to ask him politely to keep his mouth shut, is that it?" Jim asked, sipping his coffee.

"Pretty much," Gene admitted. "But I don't see that being a very productive approach. As far as I can tell, the man thinks he's pretty much immune from having his activities released and doesn't see any downside."

"What's our response, other than a pretty please?" Jim asked.

"We think that our only chance is to present him with a scenario where his name will be released to those individuals whose names he has, or may have," Gene explained. "I'm sure he'll understand that some, if not all, of those individuals would look unfavorably on his exposing them.

Especially since they probably know what's happened with the other members of the group," Gene continued. "Maybe letting our Councilman know there's a major downside to letting them know after they've previously agreed to our terms.

I'm sure he'll get the message that he has more to worry about than just his constituents," Gene finished. "He may be a big fish in the small pond down there, but he needs to understand that there are Great Whites in the water, and the blood they'll be smelling is his."

"Can't that be done with a letter to follow up the first request?" Jim asked.

"We sent a letter," Gene answered. "This guy needs a little more forceful explanation. As I first said, this guy thinks he's impervious to our threats, and I want to at least try to convince him that it's in his best interest to drop the threat of releasing the names before we take the next step."

"Okay, I get the stick and carrot approach," Jim said, getting up and heading for the kitchen. "What's the carrot? Not releasing his activities? It appears that he doesn't care about that. What else do we have to offer?"

"I honestly believe that he doesn't fully understand the lengths some of the people on our list will go to," Gene answered. "And as a final stick, he needs to understand that the Children of the Boat has a long reach if he doesn't cooperate. Basically, if the right-hand doesn't get you, the left one will."

"When do I get to meet this gentleman?" Jim asked, setting his cup in the sink.

"I'll be arriving this evening," Gene answered. "I've booked rooms for myself and the wardrobe and makeup people. The meeting is set for tomorrow morning at ten o'clock. I figure we'll have breakfast and go over the plans once more before the meeting, and you'll be done by noon."

"And am I to assume that you'll want to have dinner with Marie and me before you head back to your hotel this evening?" Jim asked, knowing the answer.

"That would be nice," Gene responded. "And it will give her a chance to ask me anything since you mentioned that she had questions about our association."

"I'll make the arrangements," Jim said. "And I'll fill you in on what I've told her before we get to the restaurant."

"Good idea," Gene replied. "I'd hate to be countering your explanations … especially since you're trying to be open about our relationship and that of the company."

"What time will you be ready?" Jim asked as the buzzer on the dryer sounded.

"How about I pick you up at six-thirty?" Gene suggested.

"I'll make reservations for seven," Jim replied, heading for the dryer.

Chapter Sixty-One

On the way to Sicilano's, Jim told Gene about his conversation with Marie regarding their assistance providing the shooter's identification and his confession regarding eliminating someone for the company.

After listening, Gene asked, "So you didn't tell her that you were the man who actually shot David's killer? Don't you think that's a shade bit evasive?"

"I suppose it is," Jim admitted. "But she never asked me that exact question, so I didn't offer an answer that I didn't know how she'd respond. I was concerned that knowing someone I had killed would make it too personal to her."

"Well, I understand your concern," Gene said as they approached the restaurant. "But now you know that you can never admit to shooting that man, or she'll start wondering what else you've misled her about."

"I know," Jim replied, shaking his head. "But I still believe that was the best way to handle it. I certainly don't think she'll start asking who I killed every time I'm on an operation for Black Water."

"Perhaps you're right," Gene agreed as they parked. "I'm going to suggest we ask her to join us in Hawaii. Sort of show her that we're not out on a shooting rampage every time we are working for a client."

"You've picked a fine mission to use as an example," Jim said incredulously. "We're heading out to sea to blow up a multimillion-dollar yacht and kill probably ten men in the process. Are you sure this is the right operation to let her see how we operate?"

"Let me handle that part," Gene said as they got out of the car. "I'll have a good cover story, complete with actors, for the part she'll be shown. I'll let you know more about it tomorrow morning while you're making the transformation to Father Sarducci."

"My friends!" Tony exclaimed as they entered the restaurant. "Come, let me show you my appreciation for the honor you've done for me."

"Good evening," Jim said as Tony hugged him. "I didn't know that bringing a known guest to your restaurant was much of an honor."

"You're too modest," Tony said and turned to Gene. "And you, sir. I understand that you're also to be held in my highest esteem."

"I'm not sure what you're referring to," Gene replied as Tony wrapped his arms around his chest. "But I'm certainly glad that I've done something to please you."

"Both of you, I am in your debt," Tony said as he led them to the back room of the restaurant where Marie, Aurora, and the twins were waiting. "Marie told me how you made it possible for the police to finally find the man who shot David. David was like a son to me. For that, I'm eternally grateful."

Jim looked at Marie and said, "I think Marie gives us too much credit. We just asked for some help from some people we know who were in a position to assist the police."

"No. You both did something that couldn't have been done without you," Tony argued. "You avenged my daughter's husband. That's a sacred honor in the tradition of my family.

Now I won't hear another word," Tony told them as he pulled out chairs for them. "When Marie explained the only reason David's killer was caught, I knew I had to make this an occasion to honor you.

Aurora, please pour all of us a glass of that special wine so I can toast these gentlemen," Tony said, walking around the table to where everyone was standing. "Then I'll go finish the meal I've prepared especially for our honored guests."

"We'd like to echo Granddad's thanks, too," Julie said, coming around to hug Jim.

"Me too," Seppa said, hugging Jim as Julie gave Gene a hug. "You're our heroes."

"We thank you … all of you," Seppa said as Julie gave Gene a hug. "You've given us something we'll never forget … an end to wondering if we'd ever get justice."

"I think you'd have gotten it eventually," Gene said as they started to take their seats. "Karma has a way of evening out the scales for everyone."

"Karma? That's a noble thought," Tony said as they toasted. "Vengeance is more traditional. And here's to the men that expedited it. They say that vengeance is a dish best-served cold. I prefer it to be served while the fire's still hot. And speaking of that, I better go get dinner while it's still warm."

As Anthony left, Gene told them. "Now, I'd like to ask Marie if she'd like to join Jim and me in Hawaii in a few days while we work on a contract regarding a new vacation resort.

Jim will be leaving for Honolulu as soon as he finishes his next trip for American and I'll be joining him the next afternoon.

It'll just be for a couple of days, but I'd consider it an honor if she'd come with me for those days," Gene added, looking at Marie.

"What about us?" Seppa asked. "We could both take a couple of days off from school."

"Yeah," Julie added. "We need a break, and Hawaii sounds pretty good!"

"I don't think you were invited," Marie told them, laughing. "But I'll take pictures."

"Pictures?" Seppa complained. "I can see pictures in any travel brochure."

"Okay, no pictures," Marie replied as Tony came in with a platter of steamed mussels and marinara sauce. "I'll just tell you how much fun I had. Now, let's just enjoy this evening, and for the record … yes, I'll gladly sacrifice my valuable time to accept this most generous offer. Just tell me where to be and when I need to be there."

"Don't expect much excitement," Jim reminded her. "This is just a working trip, and you'll be on your own most of the time."

"I think I can manage it," Marie replied. "Will I be flying commercial?"

"No," Gene told her. "I'll pick you up at Love Field in the company jet. I'll let you know in the next couple of days what day and time."

"Private jet to Hawaii," Seppa pouted. "That's just not fair."

"Life's not always fair," Aurora told them. "Let's just be happy for your mother. And thank these nice men for what they've done and what a wonderful thing they're giving your mother."

"Okay, thank you both," Julie said, disappointment in her voice. "But next time there's a trip to Hawaii, we get to come!"

"I'll make a note of it," Gene told her, smiling. "Maybe we can arrange for the entire family to join us."

"With a private jet!" Seppa exclaimed as Tony returned with a large bowl of steamed clams and cups of drawn butter for each of them.

"What's this?" Tony asked, setting the dishes down. "Since when do you think you deserve such royal treatment?"

"Since mom met Jim," Julie replied.

"I think you've created a couple of monsters," Jim said, laughing as he took a scoop of the clams and put them on his plate. "Teenage monsters!"

Chapter Sixty-Two

The next morning, Jim left home at seven o'clock to meet Gene and the rest of the team at Denny's Restaurant at the intersection of Stemmons Freeway and Regal Row, as they had discussed on the drive back from dinner.

Seeing Gene and four other men at a table for six, he walked over and said, "I see Gene has finally learned where to take his guests for a great breakfast."

"That's not exactly what he told us when we left the hotel," one of the men replied. "It was more like it's the only restaurant you can find your way to."

"Close," Jim said, taking a seat. "A man with discerning tastes always knows where to find a gourmet meal. How are you guys today?"

"Excellent," one of the other men replied. "It's always a joy to rush across the country on short notice to ply my trade. And by the way, I've had your royal robes cleaned and pressed for this occasion since I heard you're meeting a local well-respected City Councilman this morning."

"I might argue the well-respected part, but yes, I'm to meet one of the more flamboyant Councilmen of the area,"

Jim said, nodding at the waitress who arrived with a pot of coffee.

"Are you gentlemen ready to order?" she asked as she filled Jim's cup.

"We're ready," Gene answered, looking at each of the men nodding. "And I'm sure our late arrival knows exactly what he wants since he orders it every time."

"He's correct, ma'am," Jim told her as he took a sip of coffee. "I'd like the country-fried steak and eggs over medium, hash browns, and an English muffin. And a bottle of Tabasco sauce, please."

Waiting until everyone had placed their order, Jim asked, "Are we still on for ten o'clock?"

"Yeah," Gene said as the waitress left. "You're meeting him at a small coffee shop on Harry Hines. It's also a well-known hangout for the ladies who work in the area in the evenings. Some even refer to it as Councilman Pierce's primary office."

"Knowing the reputation of Harry Hines, I can hazard a guess at the occupation of those ladies," Jim remarked, nodding.

"I've also taken the precaution to have a couple of our people standing by in the unlikely event that you need assistance," Gene added. "As always, all of you will be wearing an earpiece, and we'll be monitoring the entire event as soon as you arrive."

"That's good to know," Jim said, nodding. "I'm just glad that we're meeting at ten in the morning instead of ten at night. I've never been down there, but I've heard some stories that make me wonder why anyone would be there after dark."

"I believe you know the answer to that," Gene responded as he saw the waitress heading their way. "That's the main reason for your backup. Things tend to be a little on the unsavory side in that area. Even in the daytime."

As soon as the plates were set in front of each man, the waitress asked, "Anything else, gentlemen?"

Shaking his head, Gene answered, "No, this will be fine, thank you. And would you please bring me the check when you get a chance?"

"Definitely, sir," she replied. "And I'll bring a fresh pot of coffee and leave it in case any of you want a refill."

"Thanks," Gene told her as she walked away. "Now, I'm expecting it to take no more than forty-five minutes to get Jim transformed, and it's just about a ten-minute drive from the hotel. So, there's no rush, but I'd rather have a few extra minutes making sure everything goes as planned.

Having said that, I'd like to be out of here in the next half hour," Gene continued. "And I know that Jim likes to savor his steak and eggs, but today's not the day."

"Guess I'll only have time for half of the muffin," Jim said, shaking Tabasco sauce over the white cream gravy covering his steak. "I'm just glad my dad's not here. He always said you should enjoy every meal as if it's your last."

"Then get to enjoying," Gene replied, shaking his head. "At least he's not going to tell you what he says his great - great Grandfather always said about a meal."

"Do you mean the saying that 'Pigs eat. People dine'?" Jim asked, smiling.

"Damn, he snuck it in," Gene said, shaking his head.

Chapter Sixty-Three

Less than an hour later Gene was checking every detail of Jim's now familiar Father Sarducci character and said, "You look as good as we can get it. Are you ready?"

"Ready as I'll ever be," Jim responded, looking in the mirror. "Time to meet the well-respected Jackie Wilson Pierce."

As he turned from the mirror, Gene handed him a pistol in an ankle holster, saying, "Here's a little self-protection. It's a gift from our friends at the Dallas PD with a couple of ties to some drug-related activity."

Jim pulled the pistol out as Gene continued, "It's a Smith and Wesson MP forty caliber with ten Hydra Shok bullets. The Councilman has never searched someone he's meeting, so we believe there's an almost zero chance he will today."

"And if he does today?" Jim asked as he secured the weapon just above his right ankle.

"Guess he'll have your gun," Gene answered, shrugging his shoulders.

"What if things go to shit?" Jim asked, practicing reaching for the pistol.

"That's what the gun is for," Gene replied, watching Jim adjust the position of the holster slightly. "Not to mention the two gentlemen who will be covering your back."

"Does our client understand what the impact of this operation could have if it takes a turn for the worse?" Jim asked, straightening his robe.

"We've discussed it," Gene answered. "Worst case is having a gun battle where the Councilman is killed."

"I'd argue the worst case is having a gun battle where I'm killed," Jim replied. "But let's assume I escape harm, but there are bodies remaining."

"Your backup team is carrying two kilos of cocaine and a baggie with three hundred fentanyl tablets," Gene replied. "If things get out of hand, they'll toss them around where you'll be sitting along with several hundred-dollar bills. It's rumored that the Councilman is a huge fan of recreational pharmaceuticals."

"What about the coffee shop owner? Will he be there?" Jim asked. "Or any other drop-in folks?"

"It's possible that the owner could be there," Gene answered. "But we've been monitoring the shop for a couple of days, and he either leaves or goes to the back when Jackie's meeting someone. As far as drop in traffic … it's pretty well known that when the Councilman is conducting business there, he won't tolerate any uninvited visitors."

"So, I'm going to be dealing with a megalomaniac and possibly two guards, an unknown owner who may or may not be there and may or may not be armed," Jim remarked. "Not to bring up another piece of information I'd like to have, but is our esteemed Councilman going to be armed?"

"Yes, he'll be armed," Gene replied. "His weapon of choice is a Colt model 1911 forty-five. Needless to say, it is chrome-plated with pearl handles, and he enjoys letting everyone get a glimpse of it. However, he's never actually shot it that we know of.

And since that particular pistol isn't known for its accuracy and his lack of shooting skills, we don't think he's much of a threat," Gene told him. "Hell, his showpiece may not even be loaded since it's mainly for show. But a wise man would always treat it as if it were."

"What about the backup team?" Jim asked as Gene checked the time. "How are they armed?"

"Both will be carrying Bullpup twelve-gauge shotguns with three-inch magnum shells," Gene told him. "The double ought shells each contain twelve pellets that are about the same size as a nine-millimeter bullet. Even if they're wearing vests, a close up shot from one of those to their backs will knock them to the floor.

The only issue is how fast they can be there," Gene reminded him. "Since we'll be monitoring the conversation, if we suspect any threat, they'll be coming through the door within mere seconds.

It goes without saying if you're getting concerned about how the situation is going, let us know," Gene said, putting his hand on Jim's shoulder. "You're good at reading that sort of thing, but let's be extra cautious with this guy. He's well known to come unhinged with the slightest provocation."

"Well, I guess we'd better not cause any additional provocation by being late, should we," Jim said, making one last check in the mirror and adjusting the Biretta on his head. "Maybe the good Councilman will have a sudden epiphany in the presence of an actual high priest and agree to resign and beg for forgiveness."

"You always were a dreamer," Gene said as they headed for the door.

When they reached the lobby, Gene walked to his rental and handed Jim the keys, saying, "Our guys are already in place, and they've reported that our Councilman hasn't arrived. They did a walk by and there was no one in the coffee shop at this time.

They'll let me know if that changes while you are en route," Gene said as Jim got into the black Suburban. "Let's do a final check with Quantico before you leave if you don't mind."

"No problem," Jim answered. "Comm, this is Monsignor Jim. How copy?"

"Perfect, your Excellency," the voice responded. "How me?"

"Well, I'll be damned!" Jim exclaimed. "Unless there are gremlins in the system, I'm hearing the infamous Bracer."

"That you are," she replied. "Aren't you just a little worried that lightning may strike you portraying such a religious figure?"

"Not at all," Jim answered. "I've been in much more dubious situations and survived. I think I must have a lifetime get-out-of-jail-free card. Must have been from all the good works I've done in my alter life."

"Talk about dubious," Bracer said, laughing. "Now, that's probably the best definition of the word I can think of."

"Not to interrupt this happy reunion, but we've got to get moving," Gene said. "Now, if everyone is satisfied with the communications, let's get back to business."

"Good here for everyone," Bracer responded. "Good luck, Jim."

"Good here," Jim said. "Thanks."

"Good here," came the call from the two men waiting for Jim's arrival.

"And here," Gene said. "Are the position monitors working as well?"

"Perfectly," Bracer answered. "And the feeds from the cameras we installed in the coffee shop are also online."

"Guess this is it," Jim said, starting the car. "With a little luck, I'll be back at the hotel for lunch."

Chapter Sixty-Four

"Jim, the Councilman just arrived," Bracer advised him. "Their black Lincoln Town Car is directly in front of the coffee shop front door. Your backup is parked about three car lengths behind it."

"Got it," Jim said as he turned north on Harry Hines from Regal Row. "I think I see them now about three blocks ahead."

"That's correct," she said. "Let me know if you need anything."

Moments later, Jim pulled into the parking spot behind the Town Car and sat for a moment as he looked around. Satisfied that he was safe for now, he killed the engine and got out.

Walking through the front door, he was slightly surprised to see the Councilman sitting with his back to the door and two large black men standing behind him. If he'd been the Councilman, he'd be facing the door. That is unless he had someone in the back ready to step in.

Jim walked around the table where Jackie was sitting and stuck his hand out, saying, "Mister Pierce, it's nice to finally meet you."

Jackie sat there staring at Jim for a moment and then said, "You may not think so before we're done. And for the record, it's Councilman Pierce, Father. Now sit your skinny white ass down and tell me why you're wasting my time."

Jim sat at the chair across the table and replied, "My skinny white ass is here because I don't believe that you fully understand the position you're in."

"No, I don't think you understand the position *you're* in," Jackie said sarcastically. "You folks must think I'm some kind of chump. What kind of crap are you trying to pull on me? Is this supposed to be some kind of a shakedown?

Let me fill you in on the *POSITION* I'm in," he continued as he leaned on his elbows, staring at Jim. "I told your boss, or whoever is behind this bullshit, that not only will I remain in my position within the community, but I'm going to blow the hell out of your little operation. You may think you have some power over me. But let me give you an example of my power. A few years ago, the city decided it was time to clean up the image of this area.

Well, the Police started patrolling, writing tickets, making arrests, and harassing would-be customers until it started having an impact on my business," Jackie continued. "Well, I let that foolishness continue for a couple of weeks so the Mayor and Chief of Police could point to the empty streets in the evenings and let the good taxpayers know that the city was safe for you bunch of peckerheads who want to dictate the morals of everyone.

I called the Mayor and the Chief of Police, and we had a little meeting," he told Jim, leaning further toward him. "I told him that unless that bullshit stopped immediately, I'd shut down every restaurant, shopping center, hotel, or any other business that used my people … my people … the folks that elected me."

Jackie leaned back slightly and stated, "Now, that's just a small example of the *POSITION* I'm in. I'm willing to go only so far as to let some holy roller get into my pocket. And that's exactly what you're trying to do.

You think I'm going to give up all of this because some group of folks wanted to go have a little fun in the sun?" he asked, leaning forward again. "I told you people that *MY* people don't care about that.

Now, maybe some of the other folks who took a cruise on that boat are shitting in their diapers, worried about what you are going to do if they don't follow your orders," he continued. "Not me. And if anyone should be shitting themselves right now, it's you.

You come swishing your way in your pussy ass costume thinking I even give a shit about what you want to say," Jackie almost shouted. "Well, you've gotten yourself into one hell of a situation. So, what do you have to say now, Father?"

Jim leaned back and put his hands on the table, saying nothing for several seconds, and then answered, "Councilman Pierce. I didn't come here to insult you or question your position within the community.

Nor did I come here to threaten you," Jim continued with a slight nod. "However, I am here to make sure you're aware of the ramifications if you continue down this path."

Jim paused again and said, "I'm not talking about my organization. I've already told you I'm not here to threaten you. Now, I'm not sure exactly whose names are on the list you have, if you even have a list.

But I can assure you that we have a list," Jim said, leaning forward as he put his hands in his lap. "And some of the names on that list will not be exactly pleased if you even remotely let anyone know that there is such a list.

Again, my purpose here is not to make any deals or promises that haven't already been made," Jim said, leaning back and keeping his hands beneath the table. "I just want you to stop and think what some of those people, people who hold much more power and have more to lose than you, who have been on the Love Boat, might do if they think you're a threat to them."

"You sit there all smug saying that you aren't threatening me," Jackie said, putting his arms on the table and leaning forward. "But that's exactly what you're doing. You're threatening to sic one of those pussy ass weak dick spineless folks from Washington on me. Hell, I'd have more respect for you if you would look me in the eye and make some weak-ass threat.

Now, you listen closely, Father, soon to be a dead, motherfucker," Jackie said, half rising from his chair. "You can't come down here to my turf and threaten me … no matter how you want to say it. I don't take threats. I don't make threats. I take action."

Jim suddenly stood, flipping the table toward Jackie, and dove to his right as he saw him reaching into his jacket. Pulling his pistol as he watched Jackie swing his gun toward him, Jim fired three shots as he slid to the end of the table that was now lying on its side.

As he saw the flame shoot out of the end of Jackie's pistol, he heard two almost simultaneous blasts from the doorway.

Less than a second later, he watched as Jackie's two guards fell forward, landing on Jackie's still body.

"Are you okay?" Jim heard one of the guys ask as he kept his shotgun pointed toward the three bodies on the floor.

"I think so," Jim said, slowly getting to his feet. "I'm pretty sure I haven't been hit."

Standing, Jim looked around and finally saw his Biretta lying on the floor at his feet. Stooping over to get it, he said, "Well, I guess the company owes me a new hat."

Holding the Biretta up for them to see, Jim added, "Guess Jackie wasn't such a bad shot after all. Son-of-a-bitch ruined my perfectly good fancy-ass priest hat."

"Better let me take a good look at your head," one of the guys said. "That hole in the hat looks pretty close to where your head might have been."

As Jim bent over to let him examine him, he heard the guy say, "Damn boy, you are one lucky son-of-a-bitch. There's a scrape about an inch long across the top of your head."

Jim reached up, ran his hand across the top of his head, and looked at the slight smear of blood on his fingers. "Damn, that's close," he said, staring at the blood. "Too damn close."

"Is everybody all right?" Gene asked as he heard the exchange between Jim and the backup team.

"We're good," Jim answered, looking at the bodies beside the upturned table. "Guess the score would be one scratched and three deceased."

"Are you all right to drive?" Gene asked, then immediately said, "Never mind. Let one of them bring you here in the Suburban while the other one follows the plan with the drugs and cash. And check the back rooms for witnesses. Get every camera or other device we installed. I want everyone out of there in ten minutes. And I want everyone here in my room in thirty minutes for a debrief. Understood?"

"On our way," the guy who had looked at Jim's head said. "It doesn't look serious, probably won't even need a stitch. But I'll have him there in ten minutes, and you can make that call."

"All right," Gene directed. "Let's wrap this up before the locals get there. This can still get out of hand. Move it."

Chapter Sixty-Five

As soon as Jim got back to the hotel, Gene met him and said, "Let's go to my room and have a look at that scratch."

"It's nothing," Jim said as Gene punched the elevator button for his floor. "Besides, it's a long way from my heart."

"I'm not worried about your heart," Gene replied as the doors closed. "I'm more worried about a possible concussion."

"Hell, I had worse back in Vietnam," Jim told him as the elevator rose.

"And you were twenty years younger then," Gene argued as they arrived at his floor. "And, if you don't mind my saying so, a lot more resilient. "

"I know more about how I feel than you," Jim countered as the elevator stopped and the doors opened.

"Call me cautious," Gene said as they approached his room. "Just humor me. This once for a change."

As they walked in, Gene told him, "Have a seat. I want to take a look at your head."

Jim sat on one of the couches and leaned over, saying, "Go ahead. You'll see it's just a scratch."

Gene bent over and gently moved Jim's hair to examine the area and finally concluded, "You're right. Just a scratch. But I'm still concerned about a concussion. I'm going to make a call and have someone look at you."

"Fine," Jim said, standing and walking to a mirror in the bathroom to look at the damage for himself. "I'm sure any competent doctor will agree that I don't have any problem that can't be solved with a little antiseptic.

Hell, I have some stuff at the house that Butch North gave me for minor cuts worse than this," Jim argued. "Something called Dermivet. He said he used it on a horse that tried to cut a hoof off when it got caught in a barbwire fence. And I've been using it for years when I get a little cut. Works great."

"Yeah, let's trust this to something that a veterinarian prescribes for animals," Gene said, entering the number on his cell phone.

"I want you to take the next couple of days off," Gene told him as he waited for the call to be answered. "There's a pilot we work with that will take your next trip so you can make sure there are no issues.

Hello, Doctor Jackson," Gene said as the call was answered. "I have a man who might possibly have a concussion from an accident he had this afternoon. Do you think you can take a quick look in the next hour or so?

Great," Gene responded, hearing that he could see him in an hour.

"We're going over to see the doctor as soon as I have a chance to talk to the rest of the folks from the incident," Gene said, hanging up. "You just have a seat and try to follow orders for once in your life. Okay?"

"Sure," Jim answered, resigned to letting Gene handle things.

In a few minutes, everyone from the coffee shop was in the room, and Gene said, "Okay, Jim. You first. Tell me exactly what happened."

Jim began by saying, "I started feeling nervous as soon as the Councilman began his tirade about how he wouldn't follow any suggestions. Once he said he wouldn't be threatened and started to stand, I knew that the shit was about to hit the fan.

So, I stood, lifting the table for protection, as soon as I saw him reaching inside his jacket," he continued. "So, I went to my right and pulled my gun from the holster and took a couple of shots at him when I saw his pistol.

At about the same time, I heard two loud bangs from what I now know were the backup guys taking out the two guards. I didn't even know I was hit until I picked up the Biretta and saw the hole."

Gene turned to the two backup guys and asked, "Is that about the way you saw it?"

"Pretty much exactly as it happened," the guy who had first looked at Jim's head replied. "When we heard Jackie start his tirade about being threatened, we headed for the door. Jim was on the floor firing as we entered, and we saw the two guards pulling their weapons. So, both of us fired at them."

"Same for you?" Gene asked the other man.

"Exactly," he answered. "The whole thing was over in ten to fifteen seconds."

Gene paused for a minute, looking at everyone, and then asked, "Did you get all of the equipment we had installed and toss the drugs and money down as directed?"

"Yes, sir," they answered in unison.

"Everything is in this bag," the first guy said handing a plastic bag to Gene.

Gene took a quick look into the bag and said, "All right. I want a written report by five o'clock this evening. You guys can go."

As they left, Gene said, "Now we visit the doctor, Jim. If he asks how this happened, just say that you were mowing your yard and didn't duck enough when you went under one of the small trees.

Even if he gives you a clean bill of health, I still want you to take off from the trip," he added as he headed for the door. "Just in case there are any issues… either physical or mental. Got it?"

"Got it," Jim answered, following him out of the room. "But if he clears me, I want to make my trip. I want to be well away from here when the news hits. I certainly don't want Marie to have any suspicions about any possibility of my involvement."

"Understood," Gene said as they got to the elevator. "As much as I'd like for you to take a couple of days off, I'll leave that decision to you if the doctor sees no possible reaction."

Chapter Sixty-Six

It was barely after eleven when Jim finally left the doctor's office in the medical district just off Harry Hines with a clean bill of health. Even Gene had relented there was little to no chance of any issues that would arise from the scratch.

As he was heading home, he decided to see if Marie would like to have lunch. When she answered, he asked, "Are you in the mood for some Mexican food? I hope so because I am."

"That sounds good," she answered. "Where and when?"

"Christina's there in Garland in about thirty minutes," he answered. "Maybe forty."

"Let's make it twelve o'clock," Marie replied. "I've been cleaning the house and need to do a little cleaning up of myself before I go out."

"Twelve it is," Jim agreed. "I'll see you there."

Still heading south on I-35, he decided to continue south and catch I-30 east and then 78 toward Garland. Initially intending to go home, he debated whether or not there was time enough without being late to meet Marie.

A quick glance in the mirror and he decided that going home first wasn't necessary. After the doctor had applied a small amount of antiseptic to the scratch, Jim had re-combed his hair, and the only evidence was a small, greasy-looking spot.

Traffic wasn't particularly heavy as he approached the West End Historic District and past Reunion Tower, joining I-30 just before the Convention Center District.

Heading east, he thought about the short time and distance from where he had come as close to death as he had a couple of years ago when his wife Jennifer had been killed in an attempt on his life.

Here he was, just a couple of miles from where he had shot a Dallas City Councilman and barely over an hour after having done so. Maybe that was why he had the sudden urge to see Marie. The realization that this morning could have ended much differently, and that life could be snuffed out in a split second.

The fact was he had now known Marie a little over a year and knew he enjoyed being with her as much as he had ever enjoyed being with Jennifer. Not only was it just her, but the twins and the rest of the family.

It had been a long time since he'd had much of a family. Gene and a few others were pretty much it. And that was mainly when someone needed to be eliminated. It was nice to know there were people who cared for him and enjoyed his company more than they respected his ability to kill someone with no remorse.

Possibly, the close call was the impetus that was pushing him into thinking about making his relationship with Marie and her family permanent. Maybe it was the result of the adrenaline leaving his system and the low that always followed it.

All he knew was his life was rapidly approaching a crossroads. Even his decision to let Marie know part of what his connection with Black Water and Gene involved.

Everything was starting to congeal into a more cohesive form instead of the swirling pieces of his life up to this point. But doubts still remained.

Knowing that his life could end suddenly, just as her husband David's life had ended. Knowing that something could take Marie just as quickly as death had snatched Jennifer from him.

And in less than an hour, he was going to have to lie to this same woman whom he was debating the future with. And he was going to be lying again when he met with her in Hawaii.

Perhaps Gene was right. Once you decide you're going to be completely honest, it makes it twice as hard to tell the next lie. Now that that door had been opened, it was more difficult to close it.

As he turned onto Highway 78, he still didn't have an answer … either to the question regarding their future together or how much he was going to reveal about his association with Black Water.

The closer he got to Garland, the more he wished he'd never admitted to killing anyone. But he had. And now he had to decide if he could let her know just how much of his association with Gene and Black Water was just that … assassination.

As he pulled into the parking lot at Christina's, he decided that, for now, he'd keep the extent of his involvement a secret. Maybe that was naïve of him to think he could continue to hide it, but for now, saying nothing was the best decision he could think of.

Sleeping dogs and all that.

Chapter Sixty-Seven

Ten minutes early, Jim had selected a table toward the back of the restaurant and ordered a glass of tea, saying he was waiting for someone as the waiter set a basket of chips and a bowl of salsa on the table.

Knowing how much he liked Christina's chips and salsa; he reluctantly pushed the chips away before he ate so many that he wouldn't be hungry when his meal arrived.

About five minutes later, he saw Marie being escorted to his table and got out of his seat to greet her. After a quick hug and kiss on his cheek, she sat across from him and asked, "Did I keep you waiting?"

"Not at all," Jim answered as she took a chip from the basket and dipped it in the salsa. "Matter of fact, you're a little early yourself."

"Guess I could have sat in the parking lot a few more minutes," she countered, smiling. "Just to make you wait."

"No, definitely not," Jim replied as she took another chip from the basket. "I'd have been tempted to eat that entire basket of chips. So, I'm glad you came early."

When the waiter stopped by to take their orders, Marie said, "A glass of tea and a bowl of tortilla soup, please."

As the waiter turned to Jim, he said, "I'd like the Carne Asada with Shrimp Relleno, and please substitute Borracho beans for the rice."

"Hungry?" Marie asked as the waiter walked away.

"Sort of," Jim answered, reaching for a chip. "But I'll get a to-go box for what I can't eat."

"Guess you'll have to eat it again tonight," Marie told him. "You're leaving for three days tomorrow and then for another couple of days in Hawaii with me. I'm not sure I'd eat something that's been in my refrigerator for over a week."

"Hadn't thought about that," Jim admitted. "Guess I'll be eating it tonight."

"I have a question," Marie said, pushing the bowl of salsa away.

"Shoot," Jim replied, getting another chip.

"I've been thinking about what you said regarding eliminating someone," she began. "How do you justify that? I mean, I understand the right to protect yourself.

I even understand the death penalty because it's part of the justice system. At least here in Texas," she continued. "But it seems to me what you said is outside the justice system and certainly not always a matter of self-protection.

I guess my question is, how do you justify killing someone who hasn't been found guilty of anything and isn't threatening you?" she finished.

Jim sat quietly for a minute and then asked, "How many people died as a result of Hitler's rule? What if someone had assassinated him before he was elected President of Germany in 1934? How many lives would have been saved?

He wasn't found guilty of anything, yet there were attempts on his life," Jim responded. "Would you say the man who tried was wrong? Maybe you'd have a different answer, knowing what followed when he started World War II.

But the bottom line is that seventy-five million people perished because of the failure to eliminate Hitler," Jim continued.

Pausing for a second, he then said, "Maybe it would have been wrong to eliminate someone, like Hitler, before he committed the atrocities. But let's look at Osama Bin Laden. Was he ever found guilty or even brought to court?

Does that mean that sending Seal Team Six in to assassinate him was wrong?" Jim asked. "Honestly, I have no answer to your question as to how I justify it.

I can only say that if I was sure someone was going to harm either you or your family, I'd eliminate him," Jim continued. "Is it possible that I could be wrong? I suppose so. But as much as I believe that every life is sacred, I also believe that preventing someone from taking another's life is just as sacred.

Now for a hypothetical, let's say you have proof, undeniable proof, that an organization is responsible for the distribution of fentanyl across the United States," Jim posed. "And let's say that the government has tried to get justice through the courts, but the proof was thrown out because the proof was gathered without the correct warrant.

Now further assume you had a friend whose twelve-year-old son died of an overdose," Jim continued. "Would you take measures to eliminate those people who are responsible? Or would you sit by knowing that you might have helped prevent some of the one hundred thousand deaths every year due to fentanyl overdose?

I don't know if you'd considered that justification or not," he finished. "But anytime I've been asked to eliminate someone, which is the exception to the rule, I've justified in my own mind it was necessary."

Marie sat silently, looking at Jim, and then finally said, "I guess you're right. I know that you'd never do that for purely personal reasons. And I'm not so naïve as to think it doesn't ever happen. I'm sure it's not an everyday occurrence, but I'm just as sure that it's not exactly rare either.

I guess I never really thought about it before now," she concluded. "Maybe I've had my head in the sand when it comes to thinking my government would be involved in authorizing an assassination. But after knowing about the despicable people David dealt with on a daily basis, maybe I'm glad some of them are no longer with us. Regardless of how it happened."

"Well, now that we've solved the moral issues of the day, have you given much thought to Hawaii?" Jim asked as the waiter approached.

"No more than ten or twelve hours a day," she answered as her bowl of tortilla soup was set in front of her. "And I'm still shopping for what to wear while we're there."

"Me, too," Jim said as the steaming platter was set before him. "I'm not sure which T-shirts or jeans to bring. Regarding the jeans, what do you think? Starched or unstarched?"

"I'm starting to see the reason to eliminate someone," Marie said, shaking her head as she took a spoonful of soup and blew gently across it. "But then, this time, it would be personal."

"Shut up and eat, Jim," Jim said to himself, shaking his head. "You've never learned to keep your mouth shut."

"And probably never will," Marie said, laughing.

Chapter Sixty-Eight

Jim was checking out of the hotel on the last day of his trip and waiting for the rest of the crew to come downstairs. Just as he started to turn and go to the lobby and get a cup of coffee, the clerk said, "Sir, I have a message here for you."

Turning back, Jim took the folded paper and said, "I guess I better read it then."

Leaving his suitcase and kitbag by one of the couches, he opened the message as he walked to the complimentary coffee bar. Seeing it was from Gene telling him that a car would pick him up from the terminal when he arrived at DFW and bring him to the General Aviation terminal, he wadded it and tossed it in the trash can beside the bar.

Moments later, his Captain came down and joined him, asking, "How's the coffee?"

"Just like I like my women … bitter," Jim answered.

"Maybe you should try a little sugar," the Captain said, pouring a cup and adding a couple of packets of sugar.

"Now there's a thought," Jim said as two of the Flight Attendants got off the elevator. "But then how'd I know if it was the sugar or the coffee that I wanted."

"Good morning, gentlemen," the number one Flight Attendant said, leaving her suitcase by Jim's. "Any delays getting home this morning?"

"Not that I know of," the Captain answered. "We should be landing at eleven forty-five, right on schedule. But you'll be the first to know if I find out differently."

As the elevator doors opened and the last Flight Attendant stepped off, the Captain picked up his suitcase and said, "Well, I guess it's time to saddle up and ride."

Jim gathered his bags and looked at the Flight Attendant who had asked about the delay, rolling his eyes and shaking his head quietly, telling her, "I'm ready for this trip and this month to be over with."

"No shit," she whispered. "I don't know how you can stand to be sitting beside that ass hour after hour without strangling him."

"Maybe because I'll put him on my 'do not pair with' list when we get back," Jim whispered back. "Let some other poor suckers suffer with him. One month is all I think anyone should put up with him."

A little over three hours later, as the passengers had finally left the airplane, Jim stuck out his hand and said, "Captain, I've got a guy waiting for me, so I've got to hurry on out to the terminal. It's been a pleasure. Maybe I'll see you again."

Entering the terminal, he spotted a man holding a sign that simply said 'Jim.' Walking over, Jim asked, "Waiting for me? Jim Lashley?"

"Yes, sir," the guy said. "I'm supposed to take you to the General Aviation terminal. I was told that there's a plane waiting for you."

"Great," Jim said, following him out of the terminal. "Before we go there, I need to go to the employee parking lot and grab a bag out of my car."

"No problem," the driver said. "Just point the way."

Ten minutes later, Jim had swapped out his suitcases, tossed his hat and jacket in the pickup, and climbed back into the Suburban, saying, "Guess I'm ready."

Twenty minutes later, Jim met the Captain and co-pilot of the Gulfstream that was parked just a few yards from the terminal.

"Mr. Lashley?" the Captain said, getting up from the couch as Jim approached. "I'm Sidney Jackson, and our co-pilot, Henry Robertson, is waiting in the plane. It's ready, refueled, the weather is superb, and we should be landing in Honolulu in just a little over eight hours."

"Sounds great," Jim said, shaking his hand. "Sounds like we'll get there about three o'clock."

"That's about right," the Captain said. "And please call me Sid. There are meals for you and the other five people who are already on board, and there should be a limo waiting for you when we arrive. Do you have any questions before takeoff?

"Just one," Jim said as Sid turned toward the door. "Did the company tell you I'd really enjoy two eggs over medium, a chicken fried steak covered in white cream gravy, and hash browns?"

Chapter Sixty-Nine

After setting his suitcase in the luggage compartment, he looked at the rest of the team and said, "Good morning, folks. Ready for a fun-filled vacation?"

Taking a seat across the aisle from Mischelle, he smiled at her and asked, "Did you have a good time while I was away, sweetheart?"

"Oh, yes," she answered, laughing. "But we need to get a new mailman. The guy who has been delivering the mail just isn't delivering the mail anymore, if you know what I mean."

"Guess we'll need to move," Jim replied. "The US Postal Department doesn't understand the need to swap out carriers every few weeks."

Looking around at the rest, Jim asked, "So, has anything new happened since our last meeting?"

"Gene sent this update on the crew," Rob said, handing Jim a folder. "It's got pictures of everyone, and our man on the inside says the ship has been stocked with everything we requested regarding meals and beverages."

"Good," Jim said after looking through the folder. "Anything else?"

"Just these," Larry said, handing Jim a cell phone and earbud. "We've checked in with Quantico and are online. Bracer requests you do the same before we get to Honolulu."

"I'll do that now," Jim said, putting the piece in his ear and looking at the preset phone numbers.

Hitting the speed dial number for Bracer, he waited until he heard her answer and then said, "Hello, mother. Is everything hunky-dory?"

"As hunky as it gets," she said, laughing. "Good to know you've decided to join the team. Now, this new phone uses a combination cell tower/satellite system. It looks for a cell tower, and if it can't find one with a strong enough signal, it automatically reroutes through one of the communication satellites we can access. Nothing is required on your part. You'll probably never know which system it's using."

"Sounds good," Jim replied. "And I'm sure the ones we're using are equipped with the same accessories as the others we've used."

"And some additional," she answered. "But you don't need to know what they are. Just know we couldn't be closer to you if I was sitting in your lap listening to every word and seeing what you're seeing every second."

"In that case, I better hang up," Jim said. "I'm about to get frisky with my playtime wife."

"Won't help," Bracer said, laughing. "On, off, matters not. As long as the phone has power, I'm looking over your shoulder. And you should know that the phone will stay powered for up to thirty minutes even if the battery is removed. Just a little extra insurance that we can keep track of you."

"Okay, no frisky when I'm being recorded," Jim told her. "But I want royalties when this goes public."

"That's the only drawback to the phone: the camera isn't capable of *micro*-videoing," she replied, laughing.

Once airborne and heading west, everyone rehearsed what their roles would be and looked at various scenarios as to how things might go wrong.

With one break for a late lunch, they finally decided that there wasn't much more they could plan for, and everyone sat back to relax.

Jim pulled the folder back out and memorized the faces of every crewman, from the five stewards up through the Captain. As they had surmised, there were ten people who needed to be located tomorrow morning before they could set the charges, abandon the yacht, and get back to the island.

A quick look at the suitcase he was to bring onboard, he saw it would contain a small device that was more than powerful enough to blow a hole in the side of the hull that would ensure the yacht would go down almost immediately.

Noting that the timer was set to one hour and only needed to be activated, he knew that they would need to have everyone eliminated, the entire yacht searched in case there might have been a last-minute addition to the crew, and the lifeboat ready to be lowered into the water before he hit the switch that started the countdown.

Even then, there could be no delays getting off the yacht and far enough away that there was no chance of being caught in the explosion. And he would make sure everyone else was on the lifeboat before he returned to his cabin and flipped the switch.

Chapter Seventy

As they taxied to the parking ramp, Sid came on the intercom and announced, "Welcome to Honolulu. There will be a Suburban meeting on the plane once we park and take you to the Outrigger Hotel. So please wait until I notify you the car is here before you deplane."

A couple of minutes later, as the plane stopped and the engines began to wind down, Jim looked out the window and saw a black Suburban pulling up to where the stairs had been lowered.

"Looks like our ride is here, and I've got to say, after almost twelve hours of being in an airplane, I'm ready for a shower and a cold beer before we head down to the docks," Jim announced, heading for the luggage compartment.

"Don't forget we've had just about as long in the air," Rob replied. "The trip from Quantico to DFW and this. Maybe we weren't actually flying, but sitting on an airplane is sitting on an airplane."

"Looks like we all need a shower and beer then," Jim responded, heading for the stairs. "Showers are up to you, but I'll take care of the first beer."

"There's a nice little bar at the hotel," Sid said as they started to deplane. "Called the Shore Bird. And you're in luck. Tomorrow afternoon, they'll have an amateur bikini contest."

"Damn, and I forgot to pack my thong," Larry said as he exited the plane.

"I believe Sid said bikini contest," Mischelle said as she followed him down the stairs. "Not thong contest."

"Fine," Rob told her. "I'll wear a bikini and happen to lose the top."

"If you do, I'll be in my room drinking," Jim said as they tossed their suitcases in the Suburban. "Not that you are one sexy fellow, but I've had my fill of boys in thongs to last a lifetime. Too many layovers in Miami with a few of our special Flight Attendants."

"Okay, guys," Sid said as they got into the car. "I'll see you folks in a couple of days for the flight back. Have fun!"

Thirty minutes later, they checked into the hotel, and Jim told them to meet back at the lobby in an hour so they could head down to the dock and board the yacht.

When Jim got to his room, he found a suitcase sitting on the bed and an envelope on the desk. Opening the envelope, he read the note from Gene and a key to the suitcase.

Once he opened the suitcase, he saw a collection of short-sleeved shirts with floral designs and a couple of pairs of white slacks along with some leather deck shoes.

Beneath the clothes was a false bottom that concealed the explosive, taped securely to the side of the suitcase. A blinking red light was flashing '60' over and over. Taped next to the explosive was a Sig Sauer P226 nine millimeter with a fifteen-round clip and a silencer attached. Beside it was a spare clip taped to the suitcase as well. Replacing the false bottom, Jim took out a pair of slacks, deck shoes, and a gaudy shirt with yellow hibiscuses scattered across the front and back.

After showering and changing into the tourist attire, he looked in the mirror and said, "Not my favorite look, but when in Rome …"

Thirty minutes later, Jim was sipping on a Mai Tai when Larry came into the bar. "Looks like you've gone native," he said as he signaled for the bartender.

"Gotta play the part," Jim replied as he told the bartender to put Larry's drink on his tab. "I see that you're looking native as well."

"Like you said," Larry responded as they saw Mischelle, Carolyn, and Becky walk in.

"Guess you ladies need one of the classic Hawaiian drinks," Jim said as they got to the bar.

"You are so very perceptive," Mischelle responded. "That must be why I married you."

"I thought you married him for his sense of humor," Carolyn quipped.

"And I thought you married me because I was so good in bed," Jim retorted, laughing.

"See, that's what I mean," Carolyn said, laughing with him.

"Am I too late for the joke?" Rob asked as he joined them.

"Trust me," Jim told him signaling for four more Mai Tai's. "It wasn't much of a joke."

When the drinks arrived, Jim raised his and said, "To a short but safe honeymoon, or whatever this is supposed to be."

After they toasted, Jim said, "Okay, let's get back to business. Did everyone check their suitcases?"

Seeing everyone nod, he continued, "Then let's finish this drink and find our ride to the boat. I'd like to get aboard and take a look around to see if everything is as we were told."

Just as they were about done, a man in a black suit approached them and asked, "Are you the folks that are here for the Barco do Amor?"

"Yes, sir," Jim answered. "And I assume you're our transportation to the ship."

"That I am," he replied. "If you're ready, the car is out front."

"Is everybody's luggage in the lobby, or do you need to return to your rooms?" Jim asked, setting his glass on the bar.

"In the lobby," Larry answered, looking at the nod from the others.

"Then let's grab everything and head to the dock," Jim told them.

"Just show me your luggage, and I'll get it," the driver said.

"No need," Jim argued as the rest of them set their glasses on the bar. "We'll get everything and meet you outside."

Chapter Seventy-One

When they arrived at the slip where the Barco do Amor was tied, the driver said, "Here's your ship. May I help you with your luggage?"

"Not necessary," Jim said, handing the driver two twenties. "We'll take it from here. Thank you."

As they gathered their luggage, Jim saw a man wearing a white uniform with Captain Epaulets standing at the top of the stairs leading to the boat. Leading the way, he approached the stairs and asked, "May we come aboard, Captain?"

"Certainly, come aboard, folks," he answered. "I'm Captain Eduardo Mendez, and I would like to welcome you aboard the Barco do Amor. Please call me Ed."

As they stepped onto the deck, Jim extended his hand and replied, "Good to meet you, Captain. I'm Jim, and this is my wife, Michelle. With me are Larry and Carolyn, along with Rob and Becky."

"So very glad to meet you," Ed said with a slight nod. "Now, if you wait just a moment, I'll have a steward take you and your luggage to your cabins. Then, it would be my pleasure if you'd join me on the forward deck for a drink and meet the rest of the officers of the ship."

"Sounds great," Jim replied, looking around. "This is a magnificent ship. When do we cast off?"

"Within the hour," Ed answered, signaling for the stewards who were standing to the side watching. "Once you've settled in your cabins, come to the forward deck, and I'll have the crew prepare to cast off as soon as you are introduced."

"I'm so excited," Mischelle said as a steward picked up her suitcase. "I never expected such a beautiful boat."

"Ship," Rob corrected as his suitcase was picked up by another steward. "Just remember, boats are babies; ships are stately."

"Let the lady call it whatever she wants," Ed said as the last of the luggage was collected. "Let's just call it home for the next five days."

Thirty minutes later, everyone was gathered on the forward deck, where a group of chaise lounge chairs were arranged around several small tables.

"Let me start the introductions," Ed said as they were handed Mai Tai's. "First, my Engineer, Sancho Martinez. He's responsible for the operation of all the systems.

Next is my First Mate, Ricardo Garcia," he continued as each man gave a slight bow.

"And most important for you folks, the Chef, Manuel Lopez," Ed finished. "Manuel will be preparing the meals you requested, and I can assure you there is no finer Chef to be found.

Additionally, I have stocked the ship, or boat as the lady called it, with an ample supply of the ingredients for the drinks you specified when you contracted the cruise," Ed told them as he dismissed the others. "If we happen to start running low on anything, I'll radio shore and have a boat resupply us.

Now, if there are no questions, I'll join my crew and prepare to get underway," Ed said, looking at each of them.

"Good," he finished. "You folks just relax here on the deck, and if there's anything you need, a steward will be standing by to take care of you. Oh, one other thing. The Officer's Mess will be serving dinner at five o'clock. However, if you wish for anything before then, let the steward know, and he'll make sure it's prepared."

"The Officer's what?" Mischelle asked.

"Officer's Mess, the dining hall," Jim answered. "The kitchen is called a galley; bathrooms are heads ..."

"That's all right, sir," Ed said, interrupting Jim's explanation. "We understand civilians. After all, we are mainly a civilian vessel. Now, I'll get us on our way."

"Okay," Jim quietly said as Ed left. "It looks as if there are no surprises so far. Do any of you have any questions or suggestions?"

Seeing everyone shaking their heads, he said, "Then let's enjoy the ride out to sea, have a couple of drinks, and dinner. If you want to take a look around, just be careful and don't be surprised if you run into one of the crew.

If they ask, just say you're admiring the ship or got lost looking for your cabin," he told them. "I don't expect anything except courtesy from these folks, but I'd rather not have anyone questioning why any of us are in any place other than where we're expected to be ... as a group. Or at least as a couple.

But if you do look around and see anything I need to know, let me know as soon as possible," he finished. "Now, I think it would be reasonable to have the steward bring us some hors d'oeuvres before we have dinner and retire for the night."

Chapter Seventy-Two

As arranged before heading to their cabins the night before, everyone was sitting in Jim's as they reviewed the morning's plan.

"Everyone has their guns and made sure a round is in the chamber?" Jim asked as he put the strap of a small bag over his shoulder. "And your spare clip?"

Seeing everyone showing their weapons with the spare clip, he then asked, "Are your communication pieces working?"

Again, seeing every head nod, he checked his own phone, touched his earpiece, and asked, "Can you hear me, Mother?"

"I can hear all of you," Bracer said. "How was your first night of the ménage a trois, or whatever you call it when there are six of you?"

"That would be a ménage a *sees*," Jim answered, laughing. "How can you be so pedestrian as to not know that?"

"Guess I'm just a dumbass country girl," she responded. "Now, down to business. Our cameras show the Captain and the Engineer in the Officer's Mess, the Chef and one assistant in the galley, the Mate on the bridge, and four of the stewards working on the officers' cabins.

You are anchored pretty much where we expected, and our people are standing by for you to notify us that you're away from the ship in the life raft," she continued. "When do you plan on commencing the operation?"

"In about fifteen minutes," Jim answered. "Larry, since your target is on the bridge, we'll give you a five-minute head start. Rob, you'll come with me but continue into the galley for whoever's there, and I'll take care of the Captain and Engineer.

Mischelle, you need to call for the stewards to come to the cabins as soon as we leave," Jim said. "And since all three of you are armed, just wait in your cabin until he knocks and then shoot him inside the cabin.

I think everyone needs to put two quick shots, center mass, in the chest," Jim instructed. "Then one round in the head. We don't need to waste time checking for a pulse or anything. And we damn sure don't want anyone left alive.

And then start working your way to the lifeboat," he continued. "Since you ladies are together, stay that way. We don't need someone wandering off and delaying things.

I'm going to take care of the stewards that are cleaning the officer's cabins, and then I've got to head down to the engine room to set the explosive against the hull to make sure it blows a hole in the side of the ship," he informed them. "Once I hit the switch, we have one hour to be clear. I don't know exactly how big the explosion will be, but I want to be as far away as possible.

Now, if you run across anyone unexpectedly, don't hesitate," Jim ordered. "Shoot them. Two to the chest. One to the head. Then, keep heading for the lifeboat.

Larry, since you'll have the best advantage point to see when everyone is headed for the lifeboat, keep a running dialogue so Quantico and I can both know the situation.

This is the critical stage, as you well know," Jim said, looking at each of them. "We can't have any screw-ups. I know we've been told that they won't be armed, but let's just assume they are.

And Rob, they may not have guns, but the galley is full of knives," Jim told him. "Not to press the point, but time is critical. If any of you are running into trouble, yell out.

I'll probably be the first one through with my targets, except maybe Larry," he continued. "So, I can be in the galley where the most unaccounted-for people could be within seconds of taking my targets out.

Larry, let me know as soon as you've eliminated your guy," Jim told him. "And be ready to help Mischelle and the others if they're having any difficulty.

I'm going to head down the ladder to the engine room as soon as everyone is on the deck with the lifeboat," Jim finished. "I'll give you a shout as soon as I set the device and head back up. If there's a cover or anything we need to take care of before we lower it, please do so while I'm making my way to you. Any questions?

Good," Jim said. "Larry, head for the bridge. Rob, head for the Mess, and I'll be right behind you. Carolyn and Becky, you guys go stand in front of the doors to your cabins and wait for Mischelle to signal. Shut the door and wait for the stewards, let them in, and finish them. Please let everyone know when you've taken care of your guy."

Taking one more look at everyone's eyes and seeing their determination, Jim said, "This is it. What we're here for. Remember, no hesitation. Keep communicating. And we leave no one behind. Larry, head for the bridge. We'll be taking care of our targets when you get there."

Chapter Seventy-Three

Jim waited until he heard Larry say he was approaching the bridge and then said, "Let's go, Rob. Mischelle, you guys make your calls for the stewards."

Following the passageways he knew would take him to the Officer's Mess, Jim quickly found the Captain and Engineer sitting at a table eating.

"Pardon me, sir," Jim said, approaching them. "I don't mean to interrupt you, and I know our breakfast isn't scheduled for another two hours, but with the time difference …"

"I fully understand," the Captain said. "If you'll just give us a few more minutes, I'll go tell the Chef and we'll get the Mess ready for you."

"No need for that," Jim said, pulling out his pistol. "We'll notify the Chef."

With a quick shot to his face, Jim then turned to the Engineer and placed two shots to his chest. Stepping over to where the Engineer had fallen onto the table, he shot him once in the temple and then turned, firing another round into the back of the Captain's head.

"Let me know when you've taken care of the galley," Jim said, heading for the passageway. "I'm on my way to the Officers' cabins. Larry, how's it coming?"

"Done," he answered. "Do you need me down there?"

"No, just watch for everyone to get there and let me know," Jim said, following the route he had studied to the cabins. "What's your status, Mischelle?"

"We're waiting for the stewards to get here," she answered.

"Let me know when all of you are on your way to the deck," Jim said, opening each door as he went. "I should be in the engine room within about ten minutes."

In the second cabin, which looked to be the Captain's, Jim saw a steward arranging the bed. Quickly firing two shots to his back, he stepped over and put another round through the back of his head.

"Done here," Rob called. "There was one other person with the Chef, and both are now eliminated."

"Great," Jim replied. "Now, head on up to the deck and see what you need to do to get the lifeboat ready."

Moving on down the passageway, he encountered no further people and left each door open as he went. Finally reaching the ladder that led down to the engine room, he heard Mischelle say that they had killed the three stewards who had come to their rooms.

"Good," Jim said, descending into the lower part of the ship. "Get on up to the deck. I should be there in five to ten minutes."

Just as he stepped into the engine room, he saw a man reading the gauges and making notes. Without hesitating, he walked a couple of feet closer and fired two shots into his back. As he fell, Jim stepped beside him and shot him once in the side of his head.

Looking around the area, he spotted a place where several pipes ran along the hull. Removing the bag from his shoulder, he pulled the explosive out and looked at the red number '60' still flashing.

Setting it on top of the pipes, he pressed the arming button and saw the flashing number turn solid red. Watching until it changed to '59' to be sure it was counting down, he then said, "It's armed, and I'm on my way up. Mother, I count nine targets down. What do you see?"

"That's what we see also. That should be everyone," Bracer answered. "I just sent the rescue folks on their way to get you."

"Let's hope they aren't late," Jim responded as he entered the passageway through the officers' cabins.

He hadn't taken ten steps when he saw a boy wearing nothing but shorts step out of the room where he had shot the steward.

"What the hell?" he said as he reached him. "Who the hell are you?"

"Por favor, senor," the kid said, holding out his arms. "Por favor."

"What the hell is going on?" Bracer asked. "Who the hell are you talking to?"

"Son of a bitch," Jim cursed. "There's a damn kid down here."

"What?" Bracer asked, astonished.

"There's a damn little boy standing here with snot running out of his nose," Jim answered.

"What are you going to do with him?" Bracer asked.

"I'm taking him with me," Jim answered, picking up the little boy and tossing him over his shoulder. "I'm not about to shoot a damn kid, and I don't have time to figure out anything else. I'll let you know more when we get off this damn ship, but you guys need to figure out what you're going to do with him once the rescue guys get here.

Let's get everyone on board and away from here," Jim said, getting to the deck and jogging to where the lifeboat was ready to be lowered.

Handing the boy to Rob, who was already inside, he said, "Take this kid, Rob. Just hang onto him until we're all on board."

Less than five minutes later, they had released the boat from the yacht, and Larry was heading for Oahu when Bracer called and said, "Rescue is ten out."

"Great," Jim told her. "What about the kid? How the hell did you folks miss him?"

"I don't have the answer about how we missed him, but I'm making arrangements for him to be taken to Pearl Harbor after we drop you off. That's the best I can do for now."

"You might want to have them take this kid to a doctor or something, and I'm guessing he only speaks Portuguese," Jim said, looking at the boy who was shivering with tears running down his face. "And I'd bet he's been the Captain's personal plaything, so you might pass that along.

Anyway, he's about to become your problem," Jim finished. "The rescue boat is here, and as far as I'm concerned, this screwed-up operation is over. I'm sure you'll have some answers when we get back for the debrief."

"Sorry, Jim," Bracer said quietly. "We'll figure it out, but regardless, I think you did the right thing."

Chapter Seventy-Four

Once they were dropped off at the dock, there was a Suburban waiting to take them back to the hotel. As they were slowly weaving their way through the traffic, Mischelle asked, "What now?"

"Now I take off these god-awful tourist clothes, toss them in the trash, and take a long hot shower," Rob answered.

"Let's not forget that we, and by we, I mean you, have to play a new role when Gene and Marie get here in a couple of hours," Jim reminded them.

"How can I forget?" Mischelle asked. "I have to sit there and watch my pretend husband play footsie with his real-life girlfriend."

"Well, if that's going to bother you, let's have a pretend divorce," Jim told her.

"Fine," Mischelle said. "I want my half of everything."

"That would be all right except for the pretend prenuptial agreement," Jim replied. "That's where you agreed to give me an unconditional divorce for any reason I decide and leave with only the clothes on your back."

"Damn," she said, laughing. "I wouldn't be caught dead in the clothes I have on my back right now. Can we modify the prenup?"

"Sure," Jim said. "Let's pretend none of this ever happened and just be glad things worked out as well as they did."

"That's going to be hard to do," Carolyn said. "That poor little boy. I can't imagine what he's been through."

"I know," Becky agreed. "How can any man do things like that to any child? Makes me want to neuter every male child at birth."

"I'm sorry, guys, but I don't want to continue this conversation," Jim said. "I've got to shift gears and try to forget it if I'm going to be normal when Marie gets here. I'm going to follow Rob's plan and then head down to the bar."

"Now that's a plan I can follow," Larry said.

"Good," Jim said as they pulled up to the hotel. "Let's plan on meeting at the bar in an hour."

"What about lunch?" Rob asked. "It's been hours since we ate last night."

"Say, isn't that a Denny's over there across the street?" Larry asked as he got out of the car.

"I'll be damned, it sure is," Jim replied, getting out. "But for once, I'm going to suggest we eat elsewhere. The bar supposedly has a cook-your-own steak grill."

"Not to mention that bikini contest Sid told us about," Michelle reminded them as she stepped out of the car. "I'll make a bet that you guys are more interested in the eye candy than any grill-your-own steak thing."

"Bikini, steak, grill, doesn't matter to me," Jim said as they headed into the hotel. "I just want a very tall, very strong Jack and Coke."

"Does anyone actually want to eat?" Becky asked as they headed for the elevator. "I am pretty hungry."

"I do," Rob answered. "But I still want the hot shower and stiff drink before then."

"Tell you guys what," Jim offered as the elevator doors opened. "Gene and Marie will be here soon, and I'm pretty sure they haven't had much to eat since they left Dallas.

Why don't we clean up and meet down in the bar for a drink and go over what we're going to be telling Marie about what we've supposedly been doing this morning?" he finished.

"Sound good to me," Mischelle agreed. "Maybe we can just have some fried calamari or something?"

"That does sound good," Larry said. "What time do we meet, Jim?"

"It's almost ten, so make it eleven o'clock," Jim answered. "That'll give us about an hour before you guys become the advance team for Global Resorts International."

Chapter Seventy-Five

Later, sitting at a table in the Shorebird, Gene and Marie walked in and spotted them. Walking over, Gene asked, "Do you folks mind if we join you?"

"Not a problem," Jim said, rising and giving Marie a hug. "We're just having a little drink to celebrate what I think is a great tentative proposal. That is if your boss and theirs approve."

"I guess we'll know that answer when I meet with them tomorrow morning," Gene said as Marie took the chair beside Jim, and he sat between them and Michele.

"But first, let me introduce everybody," Jim said. "Guys, this is General Gene Barker, and the beautiful lady is Marie. I'll let you figure out which is which.

And these guys are Larry and his wife Carolyn, Rob and his wife Becky," he continued. "And the odd one is Mischelle, whose husband couldn't make it."

After everyone acknowledged the introductions, Gene said, "I'm not sure if you guys have had dinner or lunch or whatever's appropriate for whatever the time is here, but I'm hungry enough to eat the south end of a northbound mule."

"We've been waiting for both of you before eating," Rob said, laughing. "This place is famous for the grill where you cook your own steak."

"Nope," Gene told him. "I'm not going to waste my time cooking when I've flown over twelve hours to get here. Let's just order from the menu and let someone else do the cooking. And as Jim always said, let me take care of the bill."

"You mean the company," Jim said, laughing. "But that sounds fine with me."

After placing their drink and meal orders, Gene asked, "What are your feelings about the contract?"

"Pretty good," Larry answered. "There were a couple of areas where I believe there's room for further negotiating, but overall, I'm satisfied that I can live with what we have."

"What are the issues?" Gene asked as their drinks arrived.

"Personnel issues," Larry answered. "Jim gave us two options regarding the security folks. Whether or not we hire local or use Black Water's people."

"What are you guys planning?" Mischelle asked after taking a sip of her Mai Tai.

"I'm sorry," Rob said. "Our company, International Resorts, is planning on building a new resort hotel with a thousand rooms, a runway that will accommodate any plane up to a 737, a road connecting the hotel to the town, and a transportation system to take our guests back and forth to the city below where we're planning to build the hotel."

"Where's it going to be?" Marie asked.

"I'm afraid we can't tell you that," Larry told her. "We're still negotiating with the country and the nearest major city. If the location were revealed, the price of the land and everything else would obviously skyrocket."

"What's your job?" Marie asked, looking at Mischelle.

"I'm in budgeting," she answered. "I take every proposal and see the impact of the estimated cost of the project. As Larry said, he's the facility security guru; there are two options regarding staffing those positions."

Marie looked at Ron and asked, "What do you do?"

"I'm the computer guy," he told her. "I have to look at how the computer systems that handle all of the operations can be designed and how much it will cost us."

"This must be an expensive project," Marie observed.

"It is," Mischelle answered. "But that's why we picked Black Water as our first choice. They've worked with us on a couple of previous projects, and we've been very happy with the results."

"I'm assuming you have all of the projected costs and what you expect from us," Gene said as the waitress came to take their orders.

"I'll have everything for you by six o'clock in the morning," Mischelle answered. "Our people are arriving late this evening, and we'll be meeting with them to brief them on the overall project. I'll provide them with the data and give it to you before your meeting in the morning."

"Excellent," Gene said. "But for now, let's just enjoy this evening. I'm sure all of you have had enough business for the day."

"And the bikini contest will start in a couple of hours," Mischelle said. "I'm pretty sure that's why the guys rushed to finish this."

"A bikini contest?" Marie asked, looking at Jim. "So that's why you go rushing off every time Gene calls."

"That and the free drinks," Jim replied, signaling for another round.

Chapter Seventy-Six

The next morning, Gene called Jim's room just a little after eight o'clock.

"Good morning, Jim," Gene said when he answered. "Get plenty of sleep?"

"Not too bad, considering," he answered. "What gets you out of bed so early?"

"It's not early. As far as my body's concerned, it is four o'clock in the afternoon," Gene replied. "And I've been up four hours talking with the folks at Quantico. Now, how would you and Marie like to join me for breakfast?"

"Hang on for a second, and I'll see," Jim answered. Seconds later, he said, "Yeah, I'll be right down, but she needs about fifteen minutes to get ready."

"And you know fifteen really means thirty, don't you?" Gene remarked, laughing. "That's fine. Gives us plenty of time to discuss a couple of things. I'm in the restaurant, so come on down."

Ten minutes later, Jim joined Gene at the table and signaled for the waitress to bring some coffee. "What's Quantico got to say about this?"

"First, that little boy," Gene answered. "He was taken from his family who live in a small town in Brazil called Alcantara by one of the local cartels. They then sold him to the Barco do Amor people.

Not only him, but his sister," Gene continued as the waitress set Jim's coffee down. "Both were taken about six months ago, as far as we can determine. The kid was a little hazy on the exact date, which is understandable.

We are trying to locate his sister so we can get both of them back to their parents," Gene said. "We believe she's somewhere around here, and I've called in several people to help with the search.

I haven't gotten the locals involved because it would be rather difficult to explain how we came across the kid," Gene said. "However, it's been less than a day, and we are making some progress.

There are rumors about a children's home on one of the smaller islands," Gene said. "Not much is known about it, but we're moving a couple of satellites into orbit so we can start searching."

"What about the operation in Brazil?" Jim asked.

"Still scheduled for a week from now," Gene answered. "But the other thing I wanted to discuss was how the overall operation here went."

Gene sat quietly for a couple of seconds and then said, "You did well. The operation itself went as smoothly as can be expected, but having that kid pop up was … well, not only unexpected but demonstrated why I chose you to lead.

Reminded me of how you acted in Vietnam when you brought all those Marines down from that hill," Gene said with emotion in his voice. "I recognized a rare man when I first saw you there, and this just shows that I was right."

"I just did what I thought was best," Jim replied. "It was nothing special, and I'm sure anyone else in my position would have done the same."

"I don't think so," Gene told him, shaking his head. "I saw plenty of guys under stress in unexpected situations while I was the Commander in Vietnam. I mean rare when I say rare."

"I appreciate the compliment," Jim said seriously. "Coming from you, it's an honor to be held in such esteem. But, next time, could you just say, 'That'll do pig. That'll do," Jim said. "What did our Senator have to say about the Councilman fiasco?"

Gene gave a short laugh and told him, "Looks like you watched Babe.

I was about to bring up that," Gene said. "Anyway, he said since news of Jackie's unfortunate event involving an obvious drug deal, people have been adding two and two and come to the conclusion that it's better to cede to the requests of The Children of the Boat than to resist.

He went so far as saying that he wished he'd had us expose a Senator, two congressmen, and three CEOs and shoot a Baptist minister. Or maybe a Pentecostal preacher," Gene said, shaking his head.

"Rumors of a 'list' have spread, and one of the major newspapers has gone so far as offering one million dollars to anyone who can provide a verified list," he continued. "By the way, you did destroy the list you had, didn't you?"

"Actually, I think it's still at home," Jim answered. "A million dollars? Sounds like a good 401 retirement package to me."

Gene gave him a look of disbelief and then said, "That'll not do pig. That'll not do."

"I'll take care of it when I get home," Jim said seriously as they saw Marie walking toward them.

"Good morning, Gene," she said, pulling out a chair. "How'd your evening go?"

"Fine," he answered as he saw the waitress coming with a pot of coffee. "Short, but fine."

"Did the lady give you what you needed?" she asked as the waitress poured her a cup and refilled the others.

"Yes, she did," Gene answered. "I had a chance to look them over and then sent copies back to the folks at Quantico. Now, I'm going to meet with the company officials in a couple of hours to discuss how they want to proceed. Then I'll fly back home, and we'll discuss it further."

"So, you're leaving today?" Marie asked. "Are we going with you?"

"No, I've got first-class tickets for both of you on a flight into DFW," Gene told her. "Your rooms are taken care of, and since Jim's pickup is still there, I figured it would be the easiest way to get you home.

One other thing," Gene continued, looking at Jim. "When you get back from your next trip, I'm sure the board is going to want you there when they wrap up their proposal on this contract."

"Shouldn't be a problem," Jim replied. "I think I have six days off before the next month's schedule."

"And, if you'd like, you can come with him," Gene told Marie, looking at her. "Give you a great chance to see Washington, DC. Monuments, museums, dinner on the Potomac. Think you can come out?"

"I'll make sure," Marie said. "Private jet?"

"See what you've done, Gene," Jim said, laughing. "Before getting involved with you, she'd have been happy to sit in the rear of the plane in the seat next to the lav."